Lorna Hill

Masquerade
at the Wells

Illustrated by
Kathleen Whapham

Piper Books

First published 1952 by Evans Brothers Ltd
First Piccolo edition published 1972
This Piper edition published 1988 by Pan Books Ltd,
Cavaye Place, London SW10 9PG
9
© Lorna Hill 1952
ISBN 0 330 02901 0
Printed and bound in Great Britain by
Richard Clay Ltd, Bungay, Suffolk

To my dear friend,
Jean Harrison, of Inghoe Low Hall,
with love

Contents

Part Three. *Pas de Deux*
Written by Mariella

Part One

Mariella Comes to Monks Hollow
Written by Jane

Chapter 1

My Birthday

IT all began on my twelfth birthday. Mummy was pouring out the coffee, Daddy was buried in *The Financial Times*, and I was thinking how awkward it is when grown-up people will persist in giving you the sort of presents they'd have liked themselves when they were your age, instead of letting you choose what *you'd* like. Suddenly Mummy stopped pouring out and said: '*Do* sit up, Jane! Really, you're getting quite round-shouldered. Don't you think so, Harold?'

Daddy just grunted from behind *The Financial Times*, and I knew by the sound of the grunt that something he'd got shares in had gone down, and that he hadn't heard a word that Mummy was saying. Mummy realized that too.

'Harold!' she repeated a little louder. 'I do wish you'd listen. It's really much more important than Peabody's Ordinaries.'

'What is?' Daddy said, looking over the top of *The Financial Times*, and I knew by the hazy expression in his eyes that his thoughts were still with Peabody's

Ordinaries, and not with Mummy and my shoulders.

'I said,' Mummy repeated patiently for the third time, 'that Jane is growing positively round-shouldered. Don't you think so?'

'Oh,' said Daddy, waking up. 'Yes, I've noticed it. It'll be all that riding, I shouldn't wonder.'

'But surely everyone who rides isn't round-shouldered,' expostulated Mummy. 'Nigel isn't. *I'm* not, am I?' I could see her looking at herself anxiously in the long mirror behind the Poole pottery bowl filled with summer flowers. Above the glowing mass of violas, sweet-williams and antirrhinums I saw her head poised – tawny curly hair cut short like a boy, long slim throat, slender sloping shoulders pulled well back. Yes, Mummy was lovely, and the very idea of her being round-shouldered was just ridiculous. Evidently Daddy thought so too, for he laughed.

'Good heavens, no! Nobody could be less round-shouldered than you, Carol. But then you do other things besides ride and pore over books. As for Nigel – well, that young man's an all-round athlete, so the one counterbalances the other, if you see what I mean. Now Jane – when she's left to herself, she reads; when she's prodded by you, she rides!'

'If I didn't prod her she'd never go out, or have any exercise at all,' Mummy retorted, sounding more than a bit annoyed. 'That's why I thought we'd get her the new pony. After all, Dapple *is* a bit stolid for a child of twelve. I can quite understand Jane not being terribly keen to ride her. Perhaps now she's got Firefly she may get on rather better.'

My thoughts flashed unhappily to my birthday present – the one Mummy had chosen for me because it was what she herself would have adored when she was twelve – the spirited, highly-bred pony, Firefly. He was tawny like Mummy, and his eyes showed just a little of the whites. Quite frankly, I was frightened to death of him. Riding fat, stolid Dapple had been bad enough, because even Dapple wasn't above shying at gaps in walls, or pieces of newspaper, but I knew quite well that Firefly would be ten times worse. I felt in my bones that even a patch of tar on the hot country road would set Firefly dancing, and as for pieces of newspaper . . . !

'Well, what are we going to do about it?' Mummy was saying. 'We can't have a round-shouldered daughter, can we?'

'Clearly some dancing lessons are indicated,' Daddy answered, putting down *The Financial Times* and sounding quite interested. 'After all, the child needs some accomplishments.'

'She's got her music—'

'Granted, but that won't stop her stooping. In fact quite the contrary, I should say. Now a few dancing lessons—'

'You mean things like the foxtrot and rumba . . .'

'Good Lord, no!' Daddy almost yelled. 'Heaven forbid! The mere thought of those languid seekers-after-pleasure flopping about on each other's necks makes me feel round-shouldered already! No, I mean ballet lessons.'

'Oh,' Mummy said rather dubiously. 'I always thought only people who went on the stage learnt ballet.'

'The old idea,' Daddy answered. 'Nowadays lots of children learn ballet just for the love of it, or to remedy various defects – such as round shoulders.'

'W-ell,' Mummy said still doubtfully. 'How do we find

out where to send her? . . . Oh, I know! What about the telephone directory – the classified part?' She picked it up off the table and began flicking over the leaves at lightning speed. 'Let me see – ambulances, anchor makers, artificial limb makers, auctioneers and valuers; 'bailiffs, brewers and bottlers – goodness! what strange things people do – cattle transporters, chiropodists, crumpet and muffin bakers – ah! here we are, dancing schools! Heavens! what a lot of places teach you to dance! How on earth do we know which one to choose?'

'Ask Irma, I should say,' Daddy answered, folding up *The Financial Times* and standing up. '*She* ought to know.'

'U-um,' Mummy said not very enthusiastically. Aunt Irma was Daddy's sister, and she was a leading dancer at a place called Sadler's Wells, which isn't anything to do with horses, though you might think so. She's quite old now – over forty – and she doesn't dance any more, but she's attached to the theatre staff. I wasn't quite sure what this meant, but I'd heard Mummy and Daddy discussing it, and I'd got the general idea. I'd also got the idea that Mummy didn't altogether approve of Aunt Irma. She always referred to her as 'poor Irma' for one thing, and for another I could see she was annoyed when people said I was like my aunt to look at. Well, now she went on absent-mindedly flicking over the leaves of the telephone directory with a frown. Then she said still doubtfully: 'Do you really think that's necessary, Harold? After all, wouldn't any of these schools do? It's not as if Jane were going to take up dancing seriously. Of course, she'll be a veterinary surgeon when she grows up, or a dog-breeder, or something. The dancing is really quite unimportant as long as it straightens her shoulders.'

12

'Well, I always believe in getting the best teaching for everything,' Daddy put in – he was now standing by the door, and I knew he was thinking he'd be late for the office. 'It's cheaper in the end, and one never knows how things will turn out. You'd better drop a line to Irma and ask her advice. Oh, and why not ask her when she's going to find time to pay Monks Hollow a visit? She hasn't been here for years and years. This excuse of always being far too busy just won't hold water now she isn't dancing.'

'All right,' Mummy said, but I could see that the idea of a visit, however short, from Aunt Irma wasn't her idea of bliss. 'I'll ask her. By the way, she's got a small child, hasn't she? A girl with an odd name.'

'Mariella,' Daddy said from the hall where he was shrugging on his Burberry. 'She's not so small now, you know. She'll be – let me see, why, she must be twelve, the same age as Jane. You'd better include the kid in the invitation.'

'I will,' Mummy promised. 'But I expect she'll be too busy. I seem to remember she's training for the stage, or something. Goodbye, and don't *scorch*, Harold – even if you are a bit late.'

'It's obvious that you've no notion of the life of a busy importer!' laughed Daddy. 'If I'm not at the office at the proper time, how can I expect other people to be?'

'Well, you won't be at the office at all, if you're lying dead in the ditch,' retorted Mummy, getting the last word as usual.

When Daddy had gone, we went on with our breakfast. At least Mummy had a third cup of coffee, and I nibbled a bit of toast and looked at my presents. Most of them

13

were things to do with horses – such as hoof picks, tail-bandages, and various bits of grooming kit that people imagined I'd like awfully. Someone had sent me a *Horse-lover's Diary* in which I was supposed to write down where I rode to every day, what prizes I won at gymkhanas, the dates of Pony Club meetings, and so on. As I never won any prizes at gymkhanas, not even the Junior Walk, Trot, and Gallop, and all I wanted to do was forget the dates of Pony Club meetings, I didn't feel the diary was going to be much use to me. Someone else had sent me a book of photographs with a marker in the page where there was a picture of foals in a meadow – quite sweet, as long as they stayed in the meadow and I didn't have to ride them! I turned the pages idly. Some of the photographs were lovely. There was one of dark fir trees, with the sunlight flickering through the branches just as it does in the wood at the edge of our North Field. There was a picture of a bather standing poised on the top of a wet, seaweedy rock, ready to dive into the water far below. There was—

'Mummy!' I shrieked. '*Mummy!* Look!'

'What's the matter?' Mummy asked casually.

'Look, Mummy, what it says here.' I thrust the book into her hands. ' "Irma Foster, in the delightful ballet *Les Patineurs*." It's Aunt Irma!'

'Well! So it is!' Mummy exclaimed. 'How strange – just when we were talking about her!'

'What does *Les Patineurs* mean?' I demanded.

'It means "The Skaters",' Mummy explained. 'But how you can have a ballet about skaters, I can't imagine.'

'Isn't she *lovely*!' I breathed, looking at the slender skating figure. 'What dark eyes she's got, and look at the sweet little poke bonnet.'

14

'Yes, she's good-looking, certainly,' admitted Mummy. 'But of course you have to be for ballet. That's all that really matters.' Years afterwards I was to learn that Mummy was quite wrong there, but at the time I just gazed at the picture, and thought how beautiful Aunt Irma was, and wished I was *really* like her.

'Of course that photograph was obviously taken years and years ago,' went on Mummy. 'I don't suppose she's the least bit like that now.'

'N-no, I suppose not,' I said regretfully, shutting the book. 'I shall have to write to Cousin Marjorie and thank her for her lovely present; it's the nicest one I've had for ages.'

Mummy laughed.

'What? Even better than Firefly?'

'Firefly?' I repeated. To tell you the honest truth I'd forgotten all about that animal during the last blissful five minutes. 'No, of course I wasn't meaning yours and Daddy's present. I was really meaning—'

'Leave it at that!' laughed Mummy. 'I understand. And talking about Firefly, you'd better hare out to the stable straight away. Nigel will be waiting for you; you know he offered to teach you to ride your new pony. So good of him, I think. It's lucky your birthday comes in the middle of the summer holidays, and that you have a nice cousin like Nigel to take care of you.'

I stared at Mummy thoughtfully, and wondered if she knew exactly how Nigel took care of me. I remembered the time he'd pushed me into the swimming bath because I'd stood shivering on the brink, screwing up my courage to jump in. To be fair to Nigel, he *had* come in after me and offered to teach me to swim, but I had never forgotten or forgiven the push. I remembered the times

15

he'd made me ride without stirrups because he said it would improve my seat; for the sake of peace I'd given in. I had even tried to jump without stirrups, and had really done my best to follow his instructions – not to pull my pony's mouth at the crucial moment; to let him have his head; to grip with the knees, and *not* on any account to hang on by the reins. Usually, though, the moment I saw the jump rushing towards me I forgot all the things I'd been told, and gripped the reins for all I was worth. Then, when Dapple had refused, or run out, I'd have to listen with shame to Nigel's sarcastic comments on my stupidness.

'You *are* a donkey!' he would say. 'You forgot all about letting him have his head. Look! This is how you ought to do it.' Then he'd sail over the jump in fine style. 'Now, you try again,' he'd say when he came back. 'Go on! What are you waiting for! And for goodness' sake don't forget – you must let him have his head. Grip with your knees, you idiot! ... Oh, what did you want to fall off for ...'

It was awful!

'There's a gymkhana at Threestones a week on Saturday,' Mummy was saying. 'And another one at Millfield the week after that. Then there's the Pony Club rally on the 14th. Aren't you lucky! All in your holidays!'

Miserably I wished that the gymkhana people, and the officials who arranged the Pony Club rallies, would at least have their beastly things when I was away at the seaside. But alas, they never did!

'Yes, Mummy,' I said, trying to sound thrilled. After all, it wasn't Mummy's fault. She imagined she was pleasing me.

'Well, you'd better be off,' she said at length. 'And tell

16

Nigel we're expecting him for lunch, and be sure to thank him for being so helpful with your riding.'

'Yes, Mummy,' I murmured obediently as I went into the hall to collect my riding-crop. It all goes to show how sometimes your good intentions let you down. As it turned out, I did anything but thank Nigel for his help that morning as you shall hear!

Chapter 2

Nigel

UNCLE ROBERT, Nigel's father and Mummy's brother, lived at Bychester Tower, half a mile away from us. Bychester Tower was a huge old house with a battlemented roof, and acres of parkland, with a trout stream winding through it. It was crossed at frequent intervals by rough stone bridges. Uncle Robert was Sir Robert Monkhouse, the squire of the village of Bychester, and Nigel had always been brought up to think of himself as the next most important person in the village after his father, so I suppose it was no wonder he was bossy. He was only a year older than me, but he was just about twice as big. He had a shock of tow-coloured hair, a ruddy complexion, and bright blue eyes. Most people seemed to think him good-looking, but I didn't. I was too frightened of him, for one thing, and if you're frightened of a person, you don't think them handsome.

Everything that I couldn't do at all, Nigel did splendidly. For instance, he could swim like a fish, and ride like a – I forget the word, but I mean the people in ancient history. He could ride a bicycle without taking hold of the handlebars; he was marvellous at tennis. He liked riding to hounds and being in at the kill. He liked going out shooting with his father, and going round the trap with Mac, the gamekeeper. He simply couldn't understand me when I told him that hunting made me

18

feel sick, and as for trapping rabbits and shooting things ... ugh!

'I suppose you'd rather stay at home and read a book,' he said mockingly.

'Yes, I would!' I answered promptly. 'Lots rather!'

'How like a girl!' scoffed Nigel.

He didn't read anything himself except *Horse and Hound, Country Life,* and *The Farmers' Weekly.* It must have been awful for Nigel, when he went back to school and had to read *Caesar,* and French verbs, and the battles of the Wars of the Roses.

Uncle Robert was frightfully hard up. At least Daddy said he was, though Nigel always seemed to have loads of money for anything to do with riding or sport.

I was just thinking how marvellous it would have been if I could have had a nice quiet boy like Francis Gibson, who wore spectacles and stammered, for my cousin instead of a tall, bossy person like Nigel, when I arrived at the stables and there was Nigel himself.

He didn't say: 'Hullo', although I hadn't seen him since last hols. He just went on whistling through his teeth the way Jameson does – Jameson is Uncle Robert's groom – and walking round and round Firefly, my new pony, with his hands in his breeches' pockets. At last he stopped whistling, and stared at me.

'Hullo, Nigel!' I said. 'Do you like my new pony?'

'He looks OK,' he answered. 'He'll make a good jumper, I shouldn't wonder. Not too weak in the quarters.'

My heart sank.

'I – I don't think I'll try jumping him just yet,' I said. 'I think I'll just get used to him first – if you don't mind.'

19

'What rot!' Nigel said, flicking Firefly gently with his finger, whereupon the pony showed the whites of his eyes much to my alarm. 'We'll try him straight away. It isn't as if you'd never ridden before, Jane. You had loads of practice last hols. I was looking at the jumps early this morning, and they're quite OK, except that the brushwood wants renewing a bit.'

Suddenly I felt the courage of desperation.

'I'm not going to jump,' I said.

'Not going to jump?' echoed Nigel, sheer unbelief in his voice. 'You mean—'

'I mean, *I'm not going to jump*,' I repeated firmly.

'Oh, yes you are,' Nigel said even more firmly.

'I am not!'

'I say you are!'

'It's my birthday,' I said. 'I shall do as I like on my birthday, and I tell you I won't jump. Why should I if I don't want to?'

'Because I say so, and I'm a boy.'

'That doesn't matter.'

'Yes, it does. I'm stronger than you.'

'No, you aren't,' I said untruthfully. 'Anyway, I won't jump if I don't want to. You can't make me.' I made for the stable door, but Nigel sprang to stop me.

'Oh, can't I? You'll see—'

It was just at this moment that Wilfred, our gardener-handyman, appeared.

'Now then, what's going on here?' he demanded. 'How dare you hit Miss Jane, Master Nigel?'

'I wasn't hitting her,' Nigel exclaimed, turning crimson. 'I don't hit girls. I'm teaching her how to ride.'

'And I don't want to be taught,' I yelled.

'Aunt Carol says I've got to teach her to ride her new

pony,' persisted Nigel, 'so she's got to learn, hasn't she?'

Wilfred glowered at Nigel suspiciously.

'I don't know nothin' about that,' he returned. 'All I know is that it's Miss Jane's birthday, and if the bairn doesn't want to ride, she shan't ride. Now you buzz off, young man. You're too cocky by half! It's time you were off to your big school. You'll soon get all that high and mightiness knocked out of you. Now buzz off, when I tell you!'

He picked up the bucket he had come in for, and went away muttering things under his breath about Nigel and his bossiness. I knew that Wilfred, unlike most people, had no love for my cousin. I'd once heard him talking to Dora, our cook-general, about Uncle Robert being the squire of the village, and Nigel being a young autocrat — those were his own words. He'd gone on to say that our village was still under the Feudal System. I didn't realize at the time what this meant, but I know now he was meaning that because the Monkhouses have been squires of Bychester for generations, people don't mind them being bossy; in fact they rather expect it. So I suppose it wasn't really Nigel's fault that he always wanted his own way.

When Wilfred had disappeared, Nigel suddenly became quite polite.

'Jane – really, I would *like* to teach you to jump,' he insisted.

But I was well aware of the charm Nigel could turn on when he chose, and I wasn't taken in.

'I've already *told* you I'm not going to!'

'You're afraid! You're a coward!' Then, as I said nothing, he went on: 'Who's going to ride Firefly if you

21

won't? He's got to be exercised, you know. Who's going to do it?'

'You can,' I said promptly.

His face brightened; then it fell again.

'It's no fun riding alone.'

'You can ride with Mariella, then!' I burst out.

'Mariella? Golly! What a name! Who on earth is Mariella?'

'She's my cousin,' I said. 'On Daddy's side. And her other name is Juanita. That's Spanish, or Italian, or something, and although it's spelt J-U-A-N-I-T-A, it's pronounced "Waneeta".' I added this information triumphantly, glad to be able to tell Nigel something he didn't know. 'She's coming to stay with us – at least we think so. You can ride with her.'

'U-um,' said Nigel doubtfully. I think he had grave suspicions about a riding-companion with such an outlandish name.

We stood in the stable for quite a bit, saying nothing at all. Then Nigel produced his trump card.

'What about Aunt Carol? Are you going to tell her you don't like her present? She'll wonder why you aren't riding him, won't she?'

I nodded with a sigh. Once more it seemed that Nigel had won.

'Oh, all right,' I said. 'I'll ride, if you like.'

'OK,' Nigel replied, his face all smiles now that he had got his own way. 'For goodness' sake, Jane, don't yank him about like that! You'll ruin his mouth. And don't forget what I told you about...'

My birthday treat began...

22

Chapter 3

Mariella

IT was a week later when Mummy and I dashed into Newcastle Central Station with just one minute to spare, only to find that the London train was forty minutes late.

'Oh, well,' Mummy said, 'we'll have a cup of coffee in the tea-room to fill in the time. Would you like something to read? There's a new pony book just out, I think. I'll see if it's on the bookstall.'

She left me standing in the middle of the crowds of people who were milling round and round the station, while she went to inquire. After a few minutes she came back with the book under her arm. It was called *Wendy and Her Pony*, and there was a picture on the cover of a terribly wild-looking animal – all swishing tail and waving hooves. Astride him, riding bareback and flourishing a riding-crop above her head, was a dashing girl wearing a scarlet pullover. It made me feel funny in my inside even to look at it! I was quite sure that Wendy would be a horrid, self-assured child – like Nigel, only a girl. However, I thanked Mummy for her lovely present, and tried to make-believe I was thrilled with it. Fortunately Mummy was too het-up about meeting Aunt Irma and Mariella to notice that I was only pretending. Not that I expect she'd have noticed, anyway.

We spent the next half-hour in the tea-room drinking warm, muddy liquid out of chipped cups, and eating cakes that tasted of mice and sawdust, and sandwiches filled with something like modelling-clay, but labelled 'tongue'. At last the forty minutes were up, and we went out into the crowded station again, and got platform tickets.

'They'll come first class,' Mummy said. 'Irma always seems to have loads of money.'

Sure enough, when the train drew in, someone looked out of a first-class compartment farther up the platform, and said in a low, musical voice: 'Porter!'

Although, as I said, the voice was low, there was something about it that made at least six porters standing near jump to attention.

'Irma!' said Mummy. 'There she is!'

I stared curiously at Aunt Irma as she gave the porter a couple of expensive-looking pigskin bags, all stuck over with the labels of exclusive Continental hotels. I didn't remember her, as I had been almost a baby the last time she'd come to visit us.

I sighed with pure delight, because there was no getting away from the fact – Aunt Irma was lovely. Not lovely like Mummy in a brilliant, breath-taking sort of way, but beautiful all the same. She was like a drawing in black and white in her black town suit, and little black hat, with a white bird's wing thrust through it. Her eyes were huge, and velvety dark. Her hair was dark too, and very smooth, and quite natural – I mean, it wasn't permanently waved like nearly everybody's is. Her face was pale like the petal of a flower, and the only touch of colour about her was her mouth, and even then it wasn't lipstick-red, but a lovely soft pink like one of those old-fashioned roses that never open right out. She wore funny little flat-heeled buttoned boots, and the sheerest of black silk stockings.

24

I was so taken up with looking at Aunt Irma that at first I didn't see the person standing behind her – a girl about the same age as me. Of course this would be Mariella.

'Hullo,' I said rather shyly. 'I expect you're Mariella. I'm Jane. I suppose you're home from school?'

'I don't go to school,' explained Mariella. 'I get taught at home. Where do you go to school?'

'Oh, I go to a big day school in Newcastle,' I explained. 'Daddy takes me every morning in the car when he goes to the office. The days he doesn't go I have to get a bus, but it's frightfully early – the bus I mean. Do you have a governess, then?'

Mariella made a face.

'As a matter of fact I have several people. There's Ozzy; I call him that, though his name's really most impressive – Osbert Darlington, MA Oxon. He teaches me French and German; he teaches me maths, too, though they're not his subject as he keeps on telling me. He says my maths are "horrible"! It's clear poor Ozzy will never make a mathematician of me!' sighed Mariella. 'Besides Ozzy, I have a Miss Linton – Honoria Linton, MA (Hons) Cantab. She teaches me English, Latin and ancient history – I can't help feeling the latter's rather appropriate – she's pretty ancient history herself! She wears pince-nez, and a gold watch on a chain that belonged to her dear mother, and she's frightfully funny sometimes though she doesn't realize it, poor darling! I think I'm her Waterloo, if you know what I mean!'

I said nothing, but Mariella didn't seem to mind doing all the talking. As we went through the barrier she chattered on gaily: 'All day long, it's: "Mariella! Will you *please* not lean on the table with your elbows. You will

25

make them rough and hard" – Mummy's put her up to that! Or it's: "Now, my dear, how would you put into Latin this sentence: 'Having followed up the enemy's forces for several days, Caesar decided to retrace his steps and return to the city'... Now, don't say you have forgotten all the work we did yesterday, Mariella!" Did you ever hear of anything so silly as that sentence?' added Mariella as we waited for Mummy and Aunt Irma outside the reservation bureau where they'd gone to reserve seats for the return journey. 'He didn't even know his own mind, the silly creature! Well, when I've translated it all wrong, and completely forgotten about *ad* with the accusative, for motion towards, and so forth, poor old Honoria sighs and says: "I fear I shall never make a classical scholar of you, Mariella, and *please* do sit up, child! You will grow round-shouldered." Mummy again!'

'How funny!' I exclaimed. 'That's what Mummy said about *me* only last week, so I'm to have some dancing lessons soon – ballet.'

'Poor kid!' remarked Mariella. Although, as I said, she was about the same age as me, she was a lot bigger, and a lot more self-confident. 'You're in for it!'

'Oh, I'm just going to learn because I'm getting round-shouldered,' I explained, as Mummy and Aunt Irma came out of the bureau and we all walked towards the car. 'Don't you like dancing?'

'It's terribly hard work,' Mariella told me. 'And you go on doing the same steps over and over for years and years – *battements*, and *pliés*, and things. Rather batty, really!... By the way, that's a nice book you've got there. I suppose you ride lots, lucky thing!'

I sighed.

26

'Yes – I do ride rather a lot. This book is about riding.' I drew it from under my arm, and displayed the fearless Wendy astride her rearing charger. Mariella stared at it in awestruck silence for a moment. Then she exclaimed: 'Imagine being able to ride like that! Some people have all the luck. It must be glorious!'

'U-um,' I said doubtfully. 'Not so glorious if you fall off.'

Mariella stared at me anxiously.

'Look!' she said, taking my arm. 'Can I ride your pony? You *have* got one, haven't you?' Then, as I nodded, she went on: 'But don't tell Mummy.'

'Oh – why ever not?' I exclaimed. It seemed terribly odd to me to want to keep riding, of all things, dark from your mother.

'Well, you see' – Mariella looked round cautiously – 'I'm really not supposed to ride, or to swim very much. Or play tennis, or even ride a bicycle. It's for fear my muscles get too big. Of course, it wouldn't matter my playing tennis and swimming a *little*. But riding – Mummy would be scared for fear I fell off.'

'Oh, you wouldn't kill yourself,' I assured her. 'But it does give you a headache. I hate falling off.'

We had reached the car by this time, and as we got in – Mariella and I in the back seat – she whispered, so that the grown-ups shouldn't hear: 'Oh, I shouldn't mind that, but you see, Mummy would be dead scared I put my kneecap off, or twisted my ankle, or any old thing. It's terribly important when you're going to be a dancer. Really, you can't do *anything* if you're going to be a dancer. Even eating – it's: "Mariella, not too many pastries! Not too much ice-cream! *Not* those rich chocolates. You can have as much salad as you like, dear—"

27

Salad!' said Mariella savagely under her breath. 'As if I want salad!'

'But why not pastries?' I asked her, puzzled.

'Too fattening,' explained Mariella. 'Terribly bad for the figure.'

'Oh, I never think about what I eat.'

'Of course not,' said my new cousin. 'You don't have to. You aren't destined to be a dancer.' Then she sighed. 'Why was I born with a *prima ballerina* for a mother?'

I stared at Mariella thoughtfully. It seemed as if there were two of us who had to do things we didn't want to do.

'What's a *prima ballerina*?' I asked as we sped down Pilgrim Street – we were calling at the office for Daddy on our way home. 'Is it any different from an ordinary dancer? I thought everyone who danced on the tips of their toes was a *prima ballerina*.'

Mariella laughed.

'Good gracious, no! There are thousands of people who dance on the tips of their toes, as you call it – we call it "*sur les pointes*", or "on point" – but only a very few of them are *ballerinas*, let alone *prima ballerinas*. A *prima ballerina* is one of the principal dancers in the company, you see – more than a soloist. In Russia, in the olden days, *prima ballerina* was a distinct rank, and there was only one thing higher, and that was *prima ballerina assoluta*. It's like Margot Fonteyn is in the Sadler's Wells Company.'

I'm afraid I looked blank.

'Don't say you've never heard of Margot Fonteyn?' Mariella said, looking at me as if I were a rare animal in the zoo. 'I thought *everyone* had heard of Margot Fontein.'

'Well, *I* haven't,' I admitted. 'Is she a very good dancer?'

'Very good?' echoed Mariella. 'She's one of the most wonderful dancers there have ever been. She's like – well, like Pavlova, or Karsavina, or Veronica Weston, only quite different of course. Now don't say you've never heard of *them*?'

I shook my head.

'Sorry, but I haven't. Ought I to have?'

Mariella just stared at me. I think she gave me up as a bad job.

'I dare say there are lots of things *you've* never heard of,' I said, a trifle nettled. 'Things like – like – well, like point-to-points, for instance.'

This time it was Mariella's turn to look puzzled.

'Point-to-points?' she echoed. 'They sound like steps in ballet, but of course they aren't. What are point-to-points, Jane?'

'They're races,' I said with a note of triumph in my voice – to tell you the truth I was glad there was something I knew that the self-assured Mariella didn't. 'If it had been spring, I'd have taken you to one; you'd probably have enjoyed it no end.'

'Don't *you* enjoy them?' asked Mariella pointedly.

'I think they're a wee bit boring,' I confessed. 'And I'm scared for fear anyone gets hurt. People sometimes do, you know.'

We had reached Daddy's office by this time, and were waiting for him at the edge of the kerb. I took the opportunity of having a good look at Mariella. She had auburn hair, like Mummy. In fact, she was more like Mummy than her own mother, I thought. Her eyes were green, and she had a beautiful figure. She wore the loveliest clothes – even I could see that they weren't in the least like mine. I remembered Mummy once saying that Harrods stuck out a mile in Aunt Irma and Mariella's clothes, and although I hadn't understood what she meant then, I knew now, though I still hadn't the least idea what Harrods was.

'By the way, Mariella,' I said, as Daddy came rushing down the office stairs, and squeezed into the back seat beside us, 'what is Harrods? Is it a label, or something?'

Everyone laughed, and Aunt Irma turned round.

'Harrods?' she repeated. 'Harrods is an institution, my child! Harrods is all London under one roof! In plain English, Harrods is a collection of fascinating shops connected by escalators and lifts.'

'All I know is,' put in Mummy, revving the engine as we edged our way out of a stream of cars, 'all I know is, if you want to feel small and insignificant and worth nothing at all, spend the morning in Harrods! Personally, I loathe the place – from the zoo and the aquarium on the first floor, to the whatever-it-is on the top! But then, of course, I loathe all London. One has to go there sometimes, naturally, but I'm always only too glad to get away again.'

'But surely, Carol, you can't loathe *all* London?' exclaimed Aunt Irma, sounding shocked. 'What about the art galleries, and the exhibitions? What about the Albert Hall? What about Covent Garden, and the ballet?'

'The ballet!' laughed Mummy. 'I've never been to one.'

'Never been to the ballet?' echoed Aunt Irma. 'My poor darling! This must be put right at once – *at once*!'

Mummy didn't answer. She was negotiating a nasty bit of traffic at the bottom of Westgate Hill.

'Why, there's a ballet company in Newcastle this very week!' exclaimed Aunt Irma, catching sight of a poster on a hoarding. 'Not a bad one, either. They're doing *Giselle*. We must all go. Now I won't take no for an answer. I shall see about the tickets myself.'

'You may find it a bit of a job,' said Mummy, as we sped up the hill. 'I'm told that ballet is enormously popular round here. Why, I can't imagine! You may not be able to get seats, I warn you.'

'Me not get seats!' laughed Aunt Irma. Then she dropped into French as I found out she had a disconcerting habit of doing. '*Mon Dieu! Quelle drôle idée!* Leave it to me.'

Chapter 4

Confidences

NEXT morning we were up bright and early, and, after breakfast, Mummy suggested that I should take Mariella to see my birthday present – my new pony, Firefly. It was a lovely day, warm, but not too hot, and as we went round to the stables, Mariella gave a sigh of envy.

'Oh, Jane – what a perfectly gorgeous place you live in!' she said.

And suddenly I realized that it was true. Monks Hollow *was* a gorgeous place. Especially beautiful it looked in the early morning sunshine, with the folds of misty, purple moorland rising steeply to the west, and the jagged peak of Ravens' Eyrie standing out black against the sky. A sombre little fir wood sheltered the house from the cold north winds, and a field of corn, with a fringe of scarlet poppies at its edge, rippled right up to the very gates. A peaty burn leapt gurgling from the moorland above, and fell tinkling into a mossy stone trough outside the stable door. It was called the Hallow Burn, and people said that it got its name from the monastery that used to be on the hillside near. You could still see some of the stones of the latter, half-buried in the sheep-nibbled turf. They also said that Monks Hollow was really Monks Hallow, for the same reason.

The house, itself, was lovely too. It was built of grey stone. The roof was stone as well, and the heavy slabs looked as if they could withstand any number of Border raids, sieges, and burnings. On the south side of the house, all was smooth lawn, and civilized garden, but on the north, the heather and bracken crept under the gates, and wild thyme filled up the cracks in the old, drystone walls. Up to now I'm afraid I had taken my beautiful home for granted, but now I saw it through Mariella's eyes.

'Oh, the darling pony!' exclaimed Mariella, breaking in upon my daydream. 'Jane, you *are* lucky to have a pony all of your own! What did you say his name was?'

'As a matter of fact I've got two ponies,' I said rather shamefacedly. It seemed awful to have two ponies, and not be the least bit thrilled with either of them. 'This one is called Firefly, and the other one is Dapple. She's in the North Field, and she's running out all the time now, because I'm not supposed to ride her much, so it doesn't matter if she gets fat. Firefly is brought in during the daytime. Wilfred does it first thing in the morning – Wilfred is our gardener-handyman. You see, Mummy would be furious if Firefly got fat.'

'It sounds like me!' Mariella said with a sigh. 'Poor Firefly!'

She fondled the pony's neck, and Firefly seemed to like it. He stopped showing the whites of his eyes, and nuzzled Mariella's hand.

'Will you teach me to ride, Jane?' Mariella went on. 'Some time when Mummy is out of the way. I'd adore to learn.'

'W-ell—' I began doubtfully.

'Oh, say you will! I'll try to learn quickly, and not be an awful nuisance. *Please* will you teach me, Jane,' she begged.

Then, as I still made no answer, she said:

'What's the matter? You don't seem a bit keen.'

'It's not that,' I assured her. 'It's – it's only that I don't ride awfully well myself. I simply can't imagine *me* teaching anyone to ride. Nigel would laugh like anything!'

'Nigel?' echoed Mariella. 'Who is Nigel?'

'Nigel Monkhouse,' I explained. 'He's my cousin, and he's a year older than me, though you'd think he was much more than that. He lives at Bychester Tower, just outside Bychester – that's our nearest village, you know. Well, Nigel's father is Sir Robert Monkhouse, the squire, and he – Nigel, I mean – rides wonderfully. He taught me; at least he *tried* to, but as I told you just now I'm not terribly good.'

'Well, couldn't he teach *me*?' asked Mariella eagerly.

'Of course,' I answered. 'Nigel loves teaching people things. He'd teach you like a shot – that is, if you think you can put up with him. He's rather a young autocrat, though,' I added, remembering Wilfred's conversation with Mrs Jobling.

'What's an autocrat?' demanded Mariella.

'It means he likes ordering you about,' I explained.

'Oh, I'll put up with that,' declared Mariella. 'I'll put up with anything if only I can learn to ride, and if your Nigel cousin gets *too* bossy, I'll jolly well tell him off!'

I stared at her pityingly. She didn't know what she was in for! I certainly couldn't imagine any girl of twelve daring to tell Nigel off. But as it turned out, it was *me* who didn't know Mariella, as you shall hear.

'Of course it'll have to be in the afternoon,' went on Mariella. 'I have my beastly practising to do in the mornings – two whole hours of it!'

'You mean music practice?'

34

'No such luck!' Mariella told me. 'Music wouldn't be so bad; it doesn't tire you out. No, I mean my *dancing* practice.'

'But I thought you said you were on holiday?'

'I've had a fortnight,' Mariella said with a sigh, turning her back regretfully on Firefly, 'and that's all I'm allowed. Of course, I'm still on holiday from *school*, if that's what you mean.'

I was puzzled, the way she said it. She sounded as if ordinary school work was an aside — not real work at all. Yet I had always imagined that dancing was just fun.

'Well, if you really have to practise for two hours, we'd better be getting back to the house,' I suggested. 'It's after ten o'clock. Gosh! Hasn't the time flown! I expect it's with having someone to talk to who isn't Nigel. By the way, if you like I can ring him up and ask him to come over here this afternoon. Then if you really don't mind being yelled at about not sitting correctly, and not hanging on by the reins, and not gripping with the knees, or going off into a daydream and suddenly finding yourself flat on your back in a ditch full of nettles, as I've done several times, well, I expect if you don't mind all that, you and Nigel will get on all right.'

'I'm quite used to being yelled at,' sighed Mariella. 'It's: "Mariella! Pull up ze knees! ... Mariella! Keep down ze shoulders. *Down*, I say – not oop! No, do not strain zem! Turn out from ze sighs" (he means, thighs) "please, Mariella – not just ze feets! No! No! zat ees all wrong! Do it again. From ze sighs, I said! Do not displace ze 'ips – zat ees all *wrong*! Nevaire, nevaire, nevaire weel I make of you a dancer!" Sometimes I think he's right,' Mariella added sadly.

35

'Who?' I asked curiously.

'Oh, he's a little Russian who takes classes at our dancing school. We can't pronounce his name – it's Ivan Dmitoritch Stcherbakof, but when *he* says it, it sounds like breaking china, so we call him Maestro, for short. Madame loves him as her life! I suppose he has got rather a grand style. He was a famous dancer once, you know – people said he was as good as Nijinsky – but he hurt his knee and can't dance any more. He's very temperamental,' added Mariella, 'and thinks nothing of banging with his stick so hard that it breaks, and he kicks the pieces right across the room. Some of the students are scared stiff, but really he's quite harmless!'

'He sounds thrilling!' I said.

'Oh, you get used to him,' answered Mariella. 'As I said before, he's a Russian, but he's travelled about such a lot in other countries that he speaks nearly every language under the sun. Sometimes he begins a sentence in one, and finishes it off in another! His English is funny, too, because he mixes up the idioms of all the languages, and trots them out in a glorious muddle, like this...' (Mariella began to imitate her Russian instructor in masterly fashion.)

' "Mariella! I to you speak, ees eet not! Why, zen, to me do you not attend, *n'est-ce pas*? *Gott in Himmel!* Do not ze shoulders strain in zat fashion there! Eet me excruciates! Eet make me veep! Zis inattention, 'e ees somesing zat I veel not stand, no! I put my foot on him, *so*! Now you veel again wiz ze musik begin. *Uno! Duo! Tre!*..." '

'I think he sounds adorable!' I exclaimed. 'Oh, Mariella, you *are* lucky to learn from a person like that!'

'Glad you think so,' answered Mariella, shutting the

stable door firmly. 'Anyway, I'm used to being shouted at. Your Nigel won't frighten me! And now, if you don't mind, Jane, I'd better go and do my beastly practising, and get it over.'

Chapter 5

Practising

THE first thing to decide was where Mariella could do her practising. She went round the house looking into all the rooms, and I followed on behind. At last we came to the big bathroom.

'The very thing!' she exclaimed. 'I can do all the things that don't need a lot of space in here. There's a grand *barre*, too – just the right height.' She went over to the heated towel-rail that stretched all along one side of the room, and tested it, leaning on it with one hand, and stretching out one leg in front, and then round to the side and back.

'*Développés*,' she explained, seeing my puzzled face. 'They're to make your muscles strong. Look out!' She kicked off her shoes. 'I'm going to do *battements en cloche*.'

I jumped back hastily as she swung her legs backwards and forwards.

'Of course I ought to be doing *pliés*,' went on Mariella. 'It's very bad to do these other things before you've warmed up, but *pliés* are so *dull*. I think, if you don't mind, I'll go and change. I can't work in this' – she glanced down at her print dress, and I suddenly realized that, although it was just a simple cotton dress, it didn't look the least bit like mine. It somehow managed to look exclusive, despite the lowly material of which it was made.

38

'What a lovely frock!' I exclaimed. 'Where did you get it?'

'This?' Mariella stared down at it offhandedly. 'Oh, Harrods, I expect. Mummy gets nearly everything at Harrods.'

'It's awfully nice,' I said.

'I suppose it isn't too bad,' admitted Mariella. 'I'm not frightfully keen on clothes, though. I simply loathe having to try them on, don't you? Such a dreadful waste of time.'

'I think it's rather exciting,' I answered. 'But I expect I don't get as many new ones as you do.'

By this time we were back in my bedroom which we were sharing while Mariella was staying with us. Without more ado, she pulled off her dress, leaving it lying in a ring on the floor. Then she pulled on a black garment, like long stockings and knickers combined.

'Tights,' she explained. 'One's never supposed to practise without them. And this' – she indicated a garment rather like an elastic pantie – 'is a jock-belt. It's to keep them up – the tights, I mean – and to give you support, as well. Jock-belts are awful when you first start to wear them; they nip like anything! But you soon get used to them.'

On top of the jock-belt, she pulled a pair of black trunks, and after that, a long knitted black jumper with very short sleeves.

'Of course in class we wear black tunics, and cross-over cardigans when it's cold, but when I'm alone, a jumper is easier. Are you coming to watch? You can if you like.'

'Oh, yes – please,' I said eagerly. 'I'd love to, if you're sure you don't mind.'

'Not a bit,' pronounced Mariella.

We went back to the bathroom, and I watched, fascinated, whilst Mariella did what she called her '*barre-work*'. Her limbs seemed just like indiarubber as she stretched them this way and that. Finally she did the splits 'just to show off', as she put it.

'They're not really ballet,' she explained, 'but every dancer can do them. Now for some point-work.' She began to rise on the very tips of her toes.

'It's not nearly as hard as it looks,' she laughed, seeing my awestruck expression. 'The shoes are blocked, you know.' She took one off and let me feel it, and sure enough, the toes were quite hard.

'But don't they hurt awfully?' I asked her.

'Well, sometimes they skin your toes a bit,' Mariella said cheerfully. 'But you get used to it – like Maestro! As a matter of fact, I'm not terribly strong *en pointe*.'

After she had practised in the bathroom for about an hour, Mariella asked me if I could tell her where she could do her centre-practice.

'I warn you, it takes lots of room,' she added. 'Things like *grands-jetés*, and *déboullés*, and full-*contretemps*.'

'Would an attic do?' I said. 'We've some gorgeous big attics.'

'Wonderful, by the sound of them,' pronounced Mariella. 'Let's away to the attics!' She danced along in front of me, her *pointe* shoes making a clip-clopping noise, due, she explained, to the fact of their not being properly broken in yet.

The south attic proved to be just the very place we were looking for. Soon Mariella was whirling across it in a way which made me feel quite dizzy to look at her.

'*Déboullés*,' she yelled. 'Quite easy, once you get the knack. So are these.' She began turning round on one spot, standing on one leg, and whipping the other round her knee. *'Fouettés,'* she explained somewhat breathlessly, after she had done twenty or more. 'Zucchi, an Italian, was the first dancer to get the hang of them, and she made all the dancers in the Russian Imperial School jealous – even Pavlova! They're quite easy, too. You have to keep whipping your head round terribly quickly, that's all. Your head should be the last thing to turn, and the first to get back into position again.'

'I think they look most awfully difficult,' I declared.

'They're not,' Mariella assured me. 'But they're very showy. The audience just loves them! You've only got to go to *Lac des Cygnes* and hear the people counting Odile's *fouettés* in the third act. They always bring the house down with clapping. Yet some of the *pirouettes* she does are really far more difficult. They're like this.' She took up a position, feet apart, then turned rapidly two or three times. 'That was a triple. Some dancers – Veronica Weston, for instance – can do six or seven. Oh, you should see Veronica – she's wonderful! She just *throws* herself into the most beautiful positions, as if it was as easy as falling off a wall! She makes you feel that everything she does is easy. That's because she's a real *artiste*, of course. Only acrobats accentuate the difficulties. I have a special interest in Veronica Weston, because she learnt dancing at my school.'

'With your funny dancing master?' I said.

'No. She was before his time. He hasn't been at our school so very long, you see. Veronica learned from Madame herself – Madame Wakulski-Viret.'

'Gosh, Mariella! The people you learn from have got funny names!' I laughed. 'But it all sounds terribly interesting and exciting – so different from here—' I glanced out of the little dormer window of the attic at the view of solitary moors and peaks.

'Yes, quite different,' agreed Mariella, with a funny little sigh. Somehow I couldn't help thinking that she preferred Monks Hollow to London.

'Mariella,' I said, when the centre-practice was finished,' 'Can I – would you mind if I tried your point shoes?'

'Oh, not a bit,' answered Mariella. 'Here you are! Catch! I'm only too glad to get them off! They're beginning to hurt. Gosh! . . .'

'What's the matter?'

'Why, you've got three toes all the same length!' exclaimed Mariella. 'You *are* lucky! You'll be able to go on point frightfully easily. That's what you call a "natural advantage" – something you just *have*, and don't work for – like dark hair and eyes, or flat knees. Other things, like stage-craft and technique, you can acquire, but you can't make your red hair black no matter how hard you work.' Mariella tossed back her bright locks, and made a naughty face. 'Unless you dye it! Golly! You've got marvellous insteps, too. In fact, your feet look awfully strong, although they're so slender.'

'Oh, I expect that's with running about on the moors with bare feet!' I laughed. 'Look here – how do you fasten these things?'

'Like this – outside ribbon over the inside. Then twice round the ankle,' explained Mariella. 'Then you fasten them at the back in a neat bow . . . Gosh! That's marvellous, Jane! I couldn't go on point for years, and you've done it straight away. But then my feet always *were* weak.'

'How on earth do you manage to dance if you've got

42

weak feet?' I exclaimed, walking about on the tips of my toes, as I'd seen Mariella do. 'This feels wonderful!'

'Oh, well – I keep on hoping they'll get stronger,' Mariella said with a shrug. 'I do all sorts of exercises for them. As a matter of fact,' she added soberly, 'I don't really think that Mummy feels I'll ever be much good, but being her daughter, naturally I've just *got* to dance. You see, it's like a second youth for Mummy.'

I nodded.

'I know. It's like that with my riding. Mummy rides so wonderfully herself, she simply doesn't understand that it doesn't thrill me a bit.'

'That's peculiar,' said Mariella, a frown puckering her forehead. 'I've always imagined you having a glorious time with a pony all your own, riding to hounds, and all that, and now I find you don't like it any more than I really like this—' She balanced in *arabesque* for a moment, then turned it into the splits, and sat laughing up at me. 'I hate all the things I have to do. Oh, if only I could stay here' – she glanced round the attic, into which the sun was pouring, at the window framing its view of Northumbrian moorland – 'if I could just spend my life in a country house like this, grooming horses, making them look nice, mucking out stables, exercising them – the horses, I mean—'

'Well, couldn't you?' I broke in.

Mariella stared at me.

'But you can't have a job doing things like that, can you?' she questioned.

'Of course you can,' I answered. 'Why loads of people want other people to look after their horses and dogs and things. As a matter of fact, that's what I'm supposed to be going to do.'

'Oh, dear! We both seem to be in the wrong jobs,' said Mariella with a sigh. 'I suppose it can't be helped, but it does seem silly. Are you finished with my shoes, Jane? Wait till you've got to wear them. Wait till you've got to darn the beastly things!' She pointed to the half-circle of neat stitches round the toe of each shoe. 'You've got to do that to *every* pair of point shoes you buy – not when they're *old*, mind you, but when they're brand new. It's to give you a grip on the boards, besides to make them last longer.'

'Oh, I thought you did it to hide the worn places,' I said.

Mariella gave a peal of laughter.

'Yes, that's what the uneducated think! It reminds me of an exhibition Mummy once took me to. It was all about ballet, and there was a glass case with a pair of Anna Pavlova's shoes in it. Well, two old ladies were staring at them, and one of them said: "My dear, I should have thought a great dancer like that would have had a new pair every day, wouldn't you? She couldn't have been very well paid to have to wear darned shoes!" No, Jane, they've all got to be darned before ever they're worn, so now you know the horrible truth.'

'I feel I'm going to like the horrid truth!' I laughed. 'I feel I shall adore darning point shoes, and doing all the funny exercises you do, Mariella.'

'Gosh!' said Mariella, staring at me, 'wouldn't it be wonderful if *you* turned out to be a ballet dancer, and *I* turned out to be an intrepid horsewoman! Wouldn't it be a joke!'

Well, there's many a true word spoken in jest, and Mariella's words were nearer the mark than she knew at the time.

Chapter 6

Mariella Goes Riding

'AND now,' said Mariella, as we left the dining-room after lunch, 'for the riding lesson. I think I'd better put on a pair of shorts, don't you? They might look more professional than this frock.'

Even Mariella's shorts had an air about them, and so had the plain, apple-green linen blouse she wore with them. I supposed they had come from Harrods, too.

As we walked round to the stables, my thoughts flew back to the conversation I'd had with Nigel that morning on the telephone. He'd sounded quite interested when he heard that my cousin wanted to learn to ride.

'That's the one with the funny name,' he said.

'Yes – Mariella,' I answered. 'But she's not at all funny herself; she's very nice, and awfully pretty. She says she wants to learn to ride more than anything on earth.'

'Oh—' I could positively hear the satisfaction oozing out of Nigel's voice at the other end of the wire. 'Then I'll come over this afternoon, shall I? Two o'clock, sharp! S'long!'

I put down the receiver with a thrill of joy to think that, at last, Nigel had got something else to keep him busy besides me and my new pony. I felt sure that Mariella and her riding would keep him fully occupied for quite a long time!

As we reached the stables and the paddock came into view, I saw that Nigel was there before us. He cantered easily across the grass, dismounted at the gate, and stood waiting for us. He was looking very workmanlike in his fawn breeches and khaki shirt.

'Hullo, Nigel!' I said. 'This is Mariella, my cousin.'

'Hullo!' said Nigel. He stared at Mariella critically, and I knew in a moment that he liked what he saw. He liked Mariella's bright, curling hair, and her bright green eyes. Most of all he liked her beautiful, lithe figure. Bright things attracted Nigel. Perhaps that was why he didn't like me. Nobody – not even my best friends – could call my black hair and pale face bright!

'Jane says you want to learn to ride?' he said after a bit. 'She says you want me to teach you. That so?'

'Oh, yes!' said Mariella eagerly. 'I want to learn to ride most awfully. Does it take long?'

'Not if you've got a bit of pluck and determination,' pronounced Nigel, looking at me in a scornful way that I knew meant that *I* had neither of these qualities. 'And, of course, you'll have to do what you're told.'

Mariella said nothing, but suddenly, as I looked from one to the other, I knew that Mariella was just as bossy in her way as Nigel was in his, and I felt that at last Nigel had met his match. I also felt that there'd be ructions in the very near future. And I was right!

All went well for a bit. The lesson began by Nigel catching Dapple, and instructing Mariella in the art of saddling and bridling her. After this, he showed his new pupil how to mount. He made her do it many times, and Mariella obeyed without a word. I stood at the gate leading into the paddock and watched them, feeling frightfully pleased it wasn't me who was being ordered about!

Very soon Mariella was learning to trot. She caught the

rhythm very quickly, and soon she was sitting in the saddle, quite at her ease. I have to admit that Nigel was a good teacher, as long as it wasn't me he was teaching! I have to admit, too, that Mariella looked as I know I never did – as if she were really enjoying herself. Nigel had fastened a leading-rein – a long webbing strap with a buckle at one end – to Dapple's bridle, and Dapple was behaving beautifully, quite differently from the way she behaved when *I* rode her. Of course, I dare say it was partly due to the fact of having another pony trotting along briskly beside her, but I felt that quite a lot was due to Mariella herself. She certainly seemed to have the knack of horsemanship.

'You've got good hands, you know,' Nigel said approvingly, when they rode back to the gate for a breather. 'You'll do, all right.'

Good hands. Yes, that was what I *hadn't* got! It wasn't only that my hands, themselves, weren't strong and capable like Mariella's were, but that I didn't possess all the other things you mean when you talk about a person having 'good hands'. You mean the way they sit, and look, on a pony. You mean that they possess that sixth sense that tells you what your horse is thinking about, and also what he's going to do, just a second before he does it! I never knew what Dapple was thinking about, much less Firefly, but I had an uncomfortable feeling that *they* knew exactly what *I* was feeling – scared to death – and they acted accordingly! I always knew, just a second too late, when Dapple was going to shy, or when Firefly had made up his mind to buck me off into the hedge. Usually I was thinking about other things when they did it. For instance, how graceful the larch boughs were in spring, like delicately pointed fingers. Or how black the fir woods

47

looked against the pale evening sky. Or how the trees and woods, standing out, clear, in the frosty winter twilight, with Ravens' Eyrie, lightly powdered with snow, towering above, looked like one of those Japanese paintings on Mummy's tea-service – all pastel colours, greys and sepias, with a hint of blue and russet. Well, it was always at a time like this that Firefly took it into his head to do one of the things ponies do when you haven't got 'hands'. As Nigel said, I was 'daydreaming again'; and I suppose he was right.

Whilst I was thinking these things, Mariella had dismounted. She put her hand on the leading-rein, and said decisively:

'Well, I can trot now, Nigel. Take this thing off please. I want to gallop – like you were doing when I first saw you.'

'I was cantering – not galloping,' Nigel corrected her. 'I think you'd better leave the leading-rein where it is just now, Mariella. You're only a beginner, you know.'

'But I want to canter,' persisted Mariella. 'How can I canter with that thing on?'

'You aren't going to canter,' Nigel said smoothly.

'But I *want* to. I'm tired of trotting. It's so dull.'

'I thought you said you wanted to learn to ride?' Nigel remarked.

'Yes, but—'

'In that case you must learn to trot an awful lot better than you do before you canter,' Nigel said quite reasonably, I must admit.

Then Mariella lost her temper.

'Don't be so bossy!' she shouted at him. 'Take it off this minute!'

'If you feel like that, it will stay on for all the lesson,

48

and for the next too,' said Nigel, looking back at her.

'It will not!'

'Oh, yes it will.'

Mariella darted forward, but Nigel was between her and the pony. She tried to push him out of the way, but he held her back easily. Her slender arms were soft and rounded – not meant for a rough-and-tumble. Against Nigel's muscled strength they were quite useless. But Mariella had another weapon. Not for nothing had she been trained for years as a dancer. She knew how to use her legs. She drew back a little, and stared at Nigel thoughtfully.

'If you don't move and let me pass,' she said deliberately, 'I shall kick you!' She looked down at her legs with a dangerous glint in her green eyes. 'And I can kick jolly hard, I can tell you!'

'Pooh!' laughed Nigel. 'You're only a girl! Girls can't kick.'

'*I* can,' said Mariella slowly.

'You should just see Jane try to play football!' scoffed Nigel. 'It's enough to make a cat laugh! She can't kick for toffee!' He turned back to the pony, presenting his back to Mariella as he did so.

A look of determination swept over Mariella's face; her mouth set. Then she lifted one finely muscled leg, caught Nigel on the seat of his breeches, and sent him sprawling on the grass at her feet.

'There!' she said exultantly. 'That'll teach you to say I can't kick!'

As for Nigel – the look of sheer astonishment on his face was too much for me. I'm afraid I laughed out loud, and so did Mariella. But our amusement didn't last long. In just two seconds Nigel was up, and the look of fury that replaced the astonishment on his face effectively stopped both our laughter.

'You'll say you're sorry for that,' he said in a low voice that fairly shook with temper.

'Oh, no I won't! I'm *not* sorry!' said Mariella. 'You dared me to do it, anyway. You asked for it, and you got it! I won't say I'm sorry!'

'Yes, you will.' He approached Mariella, but with more care this time. He had learnt his lesson, had Nigel! He waited for the favourable moment, then seized her by the arms from behind. In another minute, Mariella was down on her knees on the grass.

'Now – say you're sorry!'

'Shan't!'

'OK. Down you go, then!' He forced her down until her bright head rested on the daisies. 'Now will you apologize?'

'No!' said Mariella in a stifled voice. 'Never.'

'Nigel!' I shrieked, running round them in alarm. 'Nigel! Stop it! You mustn't do that! Her legs are most terribly precious! She's a dancer—'

'She can be the fairy on the Christmas tree for all I care!' declared Nigel grimly. 'She doesn't get up till she says she's sorry for what she did.'

'I won't say it – never!'

'Nigel!' I begged. 'Let her get up – *please*! She might sprain something—'

He brushed me away as if I were a fly.

'I'm not hurting the kid,' he assured me. 'But she's got to learn who's boss.'

And then I heard someone approaching. Round the corner of the stable yard came two figures – Mummy and Aunt Irma! They stopped in horror when they saw the two figures on the ground, and of course, I can see it must have been a bit of a shock for Aunt Irma to see her cherished *prima-ballerina*-to-be lying on the grass with Nigel more or less sitting on her chest! She dashed forward like a whirlwind, and Mummy wasn't far behind. There was a perfect babel of voices, all talking at once.

'Nigel! You naughty boy! Stop bullying that poor child – My darling! You know I *told* you not to ride ... fallen off ... broken her leg ... I shan't! Never! ... It's all right, Aunt Carol; Mariella's quite all right, really. I know she looks funny, but ... Nigel! You naughty boy! ...'

In all this Nigel was the only person to remain calm.

'It's OK,' he said, getting up. 'She isn't hurt, or anything. Matter of fact, *I* put her down there.'

There was a gasp of indignation from Aunt Irma. Then Mummy said:

'You, Nigel? But what for?'

'I wasn't bullying her, if that's what you're thinking,' answered Nigel. 'I was just trying to make her apologize.'

'Apologize?' repeated Aunt Irma, sounding more indignant every minute. 'But why should you do that? What should she apologize for?'

But this question Nigel refused to answer. Whatever his faults, tale-telling wasn't one of them. He stood looking down at his shoes, saying nothing. Mariella had, of course, risen from her ignominious position by this time.

'I kicked him,' she announced cheerfully.

There was a horrified silence. Then the grown-ups burst out together.

'*Mariella!*'

51

'Well, he said insulting things about girls,' said Mariella. 'I wasn't going to stand for that. He hadn't bargained for a ballet dancer,' she added with a giggle.

'She's right,' Nigel said generously, 'I must admit. I did say a few insulting things. I expect I deserved all I got, but I was mad at the time.'

'Well,' said Mummy, 'I think the best thing we can do, Irma, is to go away and leave them to it!'

They went away, and we stood silently looking after them. When they had disappeared round the corner of the stables, Nigel turned to Mariella.

'Come on!' he said. 'I'll let you canter, if you like. No one can say you aren't game!'

The lesson proceeded more or less smoothly, and when we were walking back to the house afterwards, Nigel having gone home, Mariella astonished me by exclaiming:

'He's a cocky little beast is Nigel Monkhouse, but I think I like him! All you've got to do is to keep him down.'

I stared at her in admiration.

'All you've got to do—' It seemed impossible to me, but looking at Mariella, I thought that perhaps *she'd* manage it all right!

Chapter 7

We Go to the Ballet

AUNT IRMA astonished us all next morning by announcing that she'd been on the phone to the theatre where the ballet was, and that she'd got the loan of the staff box for Wednesday night.

'Not another seat to be had in the house,' she said. 'You were right about the popularity of ballet up here! By the way, I hope you don't mind seeing it from a box, Carol?'

'The height of luxury, I should say!' laughed Mummy. 'As a matter of fact, I've never been in a box.'

'Well, a box isn't really the best place to see one's first ballet from,' went on Aunt Irma. 'I should have preferred the dress circle, as they call it up here. Or even the upper circle. But, as I say, it was the best I could do. It's one of the best boxes, I think. They're doing *Giselle* tonight, and something else – I forget what it is, but it isn't classical ballet.'

'Do you like classical ballet best, Aunt Irma?' I asked. 'You sound as if you do.'

Aunt Irma laughed.

'I do, as a matter of fact. And strangely enough, nearly everyone seeing ballet for the first time prefers the classical, or even *ballet blanc*.'

'What's that?' I said.

'It's classical ballet in which all the dancers wear white dresses,' explained Aunt Irma. 'Like *Les Sylphides*, and some parts in *Lac des Cygnes*. Well, as I say, it's astonishing how newcomers prefer these ballets to, say, Helpmann's *Miracle in the Gorbals*, or *Dante Sonata*.'

I'm afraid I was a bit lost with all this talk of ballets that I had never seen, so I said:

'What about the ballet you said we were seeing tonight? *Gi* – something or other?'

'*Giselle?* Oh, it's classical dancing, but not pure classical ballet,' explained Aunt Irma. 'Classical ballet depends entirely upon the dancing and the atmosphere. It's pure dancing. *Giselle* is *demi-caractère* in parts, while in others it's nearly pure classical. But none of it is as pure as *Les Sylphides*. It takes a dancer with a very pure line, and faultless technique to dance *Les Sylphides* – a dancer such as Karsavina was.'

'What about Margot Fonteyn?' I asked. 'Mariella was telling me about her.'

'Oh, Fonteyn excels in so many roles. She's beautiful in *Les Sylphides*, but, in my opinion, she's even more in her element in a part like the Princess Aurora in *The Sleeping Beauty*, or when she's dancing the Odette-Odile role in *Lac des Cygnes*. She's wonderful in that ballet, and she's wonderful in *Giselle*, too – the hardest role for any ballerina. Margot Fonteyn is so fine a dancer that she seems perfect in any role.'

After breakfast, Mariella did her practising as usual, and I watched her. When she'd finished, she showed me quite a few steps – easy ones that she said I'd do when I went to my first dancing lessons. She showed me some that she calles *ports-de-bras*. They were lovely arm positions. She also showed me how to do *pliés*, and they were just like the knee-bends we do in the gym at school, only you had to do them more carefully. You had to be sure to turn out your legs from the hips, and not just the feet, said Mariella. It was much more difficult than it sounds, especially as you had to be sure not to bend your back, and stick your behind out when you were doing them. Then I did some *grands-battements*, which were throwing your leg up in front, to the side, and behind, without bending your knee. Again you had to be awfully careful to keep your back straight.

'I think I'd make a marvellous teacher,' Mariella said with an entire lack of modesty. 'You'd be a ballet dancer in no time if you were with me for a bit!'

After lunch, we went down to the paddock again to see if Nigel was there. He'd promised to give Mariella another riding lesson. This time Mariella had borrowed a pair of my jodhpurs, and although they were on the small side for her, she looked terribly smart in them – a great deal smarter than I did.

It was another lovely day. There was a hot sun, but a cool breeze was blowing off the moors, so it wasn't oppressive.

'I wonder when that awful Nigel will let me ride up there?' Mariella said with a grimace, her eyes on the rolling moorland that stretched as far as the eye could see. 'I'd better not suggest it, or he'll say "no" just out of cussedness!'

I couldn't help laughing. She'd certainly got Nigel off all right!

'There he is!' she exclaimed. 'Gosh! He's a wonderful rider, isn't he? Fancy being able to jump over the hedge on horseback like that! I wonder when I'll be able to do it?'

While Nigel taught Mariella, I dutifully exercised Firefly. I got on quite well, because Nigel didn't take the slightest notice of me. He was far too engrossed in the much more interesting task of instructing Mariella.

'I feel I'm getting on quite well,' she said as we walked back to the house afterwards. 'Cantering's awfully easy, after all. I wonder when I can learn to jump?'

'Oh, not for a bit yet, I expect,' I said uneasily. With a shudder I remembered how many times I had fallen off when I'd first started jumping, and I wasn't exactly keen on Mariella breaking her neck. I felt that Aunt Irma might blame *me*, although really I could no more stop Mariella doing anything she'd made up her mind to do than I could cope with a ninety-mile-an-hour hurricane, or an earthquake!

'Look out!' I said urgently. 'Keep away from the windows, Mariella! If they see you in those jodhpurs—'

'Golly! Yes, I nearly forgot.' Mariella hastily withdrew into the shrubbery until I gave her the sign that the coast was clear.

The ballet began at seven. We had all put on pretty frocks, and Mummy was wearing her best fur coat. It was rather outshone, though, by the wonderful wrap Aunt Irma wore. It was Russian sables, so Mariella told me, and it was the most beautiful thing I had ever seen. With it she wore a very simple dinner dress of black velvet, made by a person called Dior. I'd never heard of a dress-maker called that, but Mariella explained that it was a 'he', and that he wasn't exactly a dressmaker, but a famous dress designer. The dress was cut very low, and Aunt Irma wore three rows of pearls that Mariella said had been given to her by a native prince when she'd danced in India.

56

As we followed the usherette to our box, the orchestra was just tuning up. I felt a thrill of excitement. The rustle of programmes, the thud of chair-seats going down, the subdued chatter of the audience, and, above all, the exciting curtain! Who knew what was going on behind it? It was all thrilling to me. And then, just as we reached our box and had seated ourselves, there was a stir amongst the people, and a burst of clapping.

I leaned over the edge of the box to see what it was, fully expecting to find that the curtain had risen. But no – the applause was merely for a little man in evening dress who had appeared in the orchestral pit, and was now standing on a small platform, bowing to the audience.

'The conductor,' whispered Mariella. 'Hush! The overture's going to begin. You mustn't talk during the overture. The balletomanes will tear you limb from limb if you do! It's supposed to get you into the right mood for the ballet.'

The lights died down, the laughter and chatter of the audience ceased as if by magic, whilst the little conductor stood with baton poised, ready for the opening notes.

'It's rather a good orchestra,' Mariella whispered in my ear after the first few minutes.

I didn't answer. I was enthralled with the beauty of the music. I had never heard anything like this before. I looked over the parapet of the box, and saw all the different instruments, and the little conductor bringing them all in at exactly the right moment, and with such assurance too. I wondered how on earth he managed not to forget one or two of them! I mentioned this fact to Mariella under my breath, but she just laughed softly.

'Oh, I expect the man who plays the drums knows where he comes in all right. If the conductor forgot, he'd do it just the same! But this conductor looks as if he knows his job – there's a great difference, you know. Some of them seem actually to draw the music out of the members of their orchestra; others just wave their batons about in time with the music, and you feel that the orchestra would be just as good without them – perhaps better!' Mariella said all this in a very grown-up manner, and I felt pretty sure she'd heard her mother say it.

'Oh, look!' I exclaimed. 'The curtain's going up!'

The curtain had indeed risen silently, and now I was looking down upon an empty stage, with a thatched cottage at each side and a view of mountains, crowned by a medieval castle, beyond. I sat entranced while the story of Giselle's tragic love of the dance unfolded itself. The beautiful peasant girl was the personification of lightness and grace. When she was betrayed by her lover, Albrecht, lost her reason, and finally killed herself, I gripped the edge of the box in my agony.

'It's all right,' whsipered Mariella as the curtain went down. 'She comes alive again – at least sort of alive – in the next act. She becomes a Wili – that's a girl who dies by her own hand the night before her wedding.'

I hardly noticed the curtain fall, so lost was I in my dream. And then, suddenly, the funniest thing happened. Our box seemed to be full of strange people. They couldn't all get in properly, so some of them overflowed into the vestibule outside. There were quite six men in evening dress, and several women. Some of the men had little pointed beards, and most of them spoke with foreign accents. Aunt Irma was in the middle of the group, talking graciously to them as if she were somebody terribly important, like the Queen. Poor Mummy was left quite in the background, looking less assured than I have ever

The story of Giselle's tragic love unfolded itself

seen her. As for Mariella – she was talking and laughing to the visitors, as if she were quite used to this sort of thing. She seemed to take it as a matter of course that her mother should be made such a fuss of.

One of the gentlemen presented a bouquet of roses and carnations to Aunt Irma. She held it up to her cheek with the prettiest gesture, and then laid it down on the edge of the box. At the same moment, there was a sound from the auditorium – a soft, rustling sound, like wings stirring. And then I saw that all the people in the theatre had turned their heads, and were looking straight towards our box. Then they were clapping. Finally some of them rose to their feet, and then the whole house followed suit. It was thrilling! I felt as if we were royalty!

Aunt Irma went to the side of the box, bowed to the people, and then kissed her hand to them. They went on clapping and stamping so that she had to keep on doing it, until I began to wonder if she'd have to go on kissing her hand and bowing all night! Fortunately, though, the lights went down, the curtain rose, and the next act began. When I turned round, the bowing, hand-kissing gentlemen, and the strange women had vanished like a dream.

I loved the second act of *Giselle* even more than the first. The strange phantom-like Wilis, with their floating veils, filled me with enchantment. I felt all Albrecht's sorrow as he knelt beside the grave of Giselle, his beloved, and laid upon it his sheaf of lilies. I felt his amazement when he beheld her as one of those strange, wraith-like phantoms of the woods – a Wili. I shared the Prince's despair when, having begged in vain for mercy of Myrtha, cruel Queen of the Wilis, he was condemned by her to dance to his death.

60

I'm afraid I was thinking so much about *Giselle* that I hardly noticed the second ballet presented by the company. As Aunt Irma had said, it was a modern work, and I have no doubt that it was all very clever, but it just didn't appeal to me. As I sat watching the flowing dresses of the dancers, I was still in the forest glade with Giselle and her wraith-like companions.

Going home in the car, I thought about the ballet, and as we drove under the sweeping boughs of the fir woods, I saw again those white dancing figures, light as thistle-down, ethereal as the wreaths of mist hanging in the branches and drifting in the hollows of the wood.

'*Jane!*' came Mariella's voice out of the darkness. 'Jane, do you ever hunt? Do wake up, Jane! I said do you ever hunt? I think hunting must be the most marvellous fun!'

My dream was shattered. Hunting! The meet at Monks Hollow flashed before my eyes – the flickering white and tan of the foxhounds, the creaking of leather, the jingle of flashing steel bits and bridles, the snowy stocks and immaculate breeches of the followers, the hunting pink of the members – I saw it all! I saw the scene a few hours later – tired horses, mud-bespattered horsemen, tales of the fox they'd raised in Hunters' Copse – the fox that had given them such a good run ... 'Right over Corbie Fell, my dear, and down into that patch of woody ground near Bychester Tower. Lost him right over in the west by Ravens' Corrie. Grand day's sport!'

Tales of the fox that had gone to earth not far from Monks Hollow. They'd dug him out ... I refused even to think of it.

61

'Do you think the fox *likes* to be hunted?' came Mariella's voice again.

'The people who hunt say so!' I answered sarcastically.

Mariella missed the sarcasm.

'I expect you're right. I should think he probably does. After all, people pay no end of money just to get a thrill – even if it *is* dangerous – like climbing the Matterhorn, or finding the South Pole, or tobogganing down the Cresta Run in Switzerland. And the fox gets it all for nothing.'

'—um,' I said doubtfully. 'Look, Mariella! This little stone cottage reminds me of the one in *Giselle* – the one Giselle's mother lived in.'

'*Giselle?*' echoed Mariella. 'Oh, yes – of course. I'd forgotten about it for the moment... This must be marvellous country to ride over, Jane – all open, miles and miles of it.'

'Yes,' I answered. 'It *is* pretty open. In fact, north of us, it just goes on and on, right up to the border.'

After this, we were both silent. I went back to my thoughts of *Giselle*, and I'm pretty sure Mariella was thinking about tomorrow's riding lesson with Nigel. Mummy and Aunt Irma talked softly to each other about all sorts of things, and I heard Mummy thanking Aunt Irma for a very pleasant evening. I couldn't help thinking how wonderful grown-up people are at disguising their feelings, because I'm pretty sure Mummy had been dreadfully bored! As for me, 'pleasant evening' didn't describe my feelings at all. For me the evening had been like the raising of a curtain that had shown me something I hadn't known existed – an enchanted land. Somehow I knew by instinct that this evening was going to change my whole life.

62

Chapter 8

Borcovicus

'WHAT about a ride today,' Nigel suggested. We were all sitting in the hay-loft above the stable, Nigel having ridden over straight after lunch as he had done ever since Mariella had come to stay. 'Couldn't we have a picnic somewhere?'

'What a lovely idea!' exclaimed Mariella. 'But where could we have it?'

'How about the Monks' Pool, near Bliss Castle?' I said. 'It's a gorgeous place, and we could bathe.'

'I was there last week with Richard Lister,' said Nigel. 'I vote we go somewhere fresh. What about Borcovicus? We could ride there, and it would be practice for Mariella.'

'What a funny name?' said Mariella. 'It doesn't sound English.'

'It isn't,' answered Nigel. 'It's Roman. Borcovicus is a Roman camp. It's sometimes called Borcovicum, and in English it's Housesteads. Well, I vote we ride over there and have a look round. It's a grand place!'

'Is it very far?' Mariella wanted to know.

'About five miles – just a nice little ride for you,' Nigel replied, a trifle patronizingly, I thought. But Mariella didn't seem to mind.

'Yes, let's do that!' she said enthusiastically. 'What about the tea? Could we go up to the house and beg some, do you think, Jane?'

'Yes, of course,' I said. 'I expect they'll be only too glad to get rid of us!'

We saddled up the ponies, and packed our haversacks with provisions – packets of sandwiches, slabs of fruit cake, and two bottles of lemonade. We didn't bother about cups, because, as Nigel said, we could drink out of the bottle, turn and turn about.

'Be sure to take your macs!' Mummy yelled after us, as we trotted out of the stable yard. 'It looks like rain!'

'Too windy!' Nigel yelled back! Then he reined in Max, his pony, and added: 'OK, Aunt Carol. We'll come back for them! You two ride on, and I'll go up to the house for the blessed things. I'll catch you up. Why must you have people who *fuss* for parents, Jane?'

'Mummy doesn't fuss; it does look like rain,' I retorted indignantly, but Nigel was already out of earshot.

'I must say it's decent of him to go back and save us the trouble,' remarked Mariella. 'Really, I like Nigel awfully. The more I see of him, the more I like him.'

I said nothing. When you dislike a person as much as I dislike Nigel, it's best not to say so. After all, it doesn't do any good.

It wasn't long before Nigel caught us up.

'Here you are!' he yelled. 'Catch!' He flung Mariella's mackintosh to her, and the other in my direction. 'Look out, Jane! ... You should have known he'd shy! ... Oh, never mind! I'll catch him. Really, you *are* a little nuisance!'

As I picked myself out of a tangle of blackberry bushes that were growing by the side of the road, I made a mental resolution that, when I was grown up, I would never, never sit on a horse's back again. There would be no Nigel in those glorious far-off days to boss me and tell me to: 'Get on, and be quick about it! We've wasted half an hour already over your stupid mac and your bad management of Firefly.'

We rode on, Mariella and Nigel chattering like a couple of magpies, me in silence just a little way behind. It was frightfully boring. I couldn't even daydream, as I did when I rode Dapple, because the moment you took your mind off Firefly, he knew it, and did something awful!

About half past three we arrived at the wicket-gate leading into the mile or so of moorland that stretches up to the ancient Roman camp of Borcovicus. The turf was soft and springy and studded all over with the tiniest of white flowers – almost like moss. Even *I* enjoyed the canter up the hill to the next gate. Firefly was a lovely smooth 'ride' – a great deal more comfortable than Dapple.

We had been riding along the Military Road, that runs east and west from Newcastle to Carlisle mostly by the side of the old Roman Wall, but sometimes right on top of it, and all the time the wind had been rising. Now, in this exposed place, it reached gale force. The grey clouds billowed over our heads like gigantic balloons made of sailcloth, and every now and then a spatter of rain and hail hit us in the face like a handful of tiny glass pebbles. The ponies didn't like it a bit, and laid back their ears and side-stepped along. I couldn't help thinking that it was a fitting day for such a wild and desolate spot. It didn't take much imagination to hear the wolves howling round the gates of the Roman encampment! Coming back to everyday things, I was glad that Mummy had insisted upon the macs. There wasn't a particle of shelter up here on these lonely hills, and the sky was becoming darker every minute. If it really *did* rain, we'd be drenched in no time. Not that Nigel would care, I reflected bitterly. He was as hard as nails, and quite used to getting wet through to the skin on a day in the hunting field.

We met quite a few people hurrying down from the camp, all anxious to get away in their cars before the storm really began. When we reached the walled-in enclosure, it was quite deserted – not a soul in sight except ourselves. Even the man who took your money at the gate was just hurrying away to wherever it was he lived, a torn bit of mackintosh over his head to protect him from the wind. He peered at us from underneath it, as if he thought we were quite batty, when Nigel asked if we could tie our ponies up to the gate.

'Oh, aye,' he said. 'There'll no be mony folk i' the place this evenin'. It's tanpence apiece ye'll be owing me.'

Nigel paid the tenpences. I took mine out of my pocket and gave it to him, but Mariella let him pay, although I knew she had a great deal more pocket money than he had!

When we were inside the enclosure, Nigel conducted us round in lordly fashion, and I must say he seemed to know quite a lot about it. He pointed out the south gateway, showing us the grooves worn by the wheels of the Roman chariots.

'Reminds me of the Indian song: "Less than the dust beneath thy chariot wheel!"' He laughed. 'You know – the one that ghastly female sang at the parish concert last Christmas. I imagine that would express to a "t" the feelings of those Roman johnnies towards their English and Scottish captives! By the way – here's the bath they used to wash 'em in.'

66

'They *didn't*, Nigel!' giggled Mariella.

'Yes, they did – honest injin!' persisted Nigel. 'Clean fellows, those Romans! They weren't going to have a lot of filthy, stinking Britons among them – even in their dungeons! So, on arrival they dipped 'em like a lot of sheep! And this is the same old tub!' He kicked it with his riding-boot. 'You can still see the plug-hole. When those Roman johnnies made a thing, they made it to last! Oh, and over there' – he pointed with his riding-crop at a small stone enclosure outside the main walls – 'is what is known as the Murder House. Umpteen skeletons were unearthed in it. Some women, too! Gosh! They knew how to treat women in those days!' He gave Mariella a sidelong look, but she didn't rise to the bait.

We had tea sitting behind a wall in one of the little stone guard-houses. It was fairly sheltered behind the stout walls, and the rain seemed to have stopped so we were quite comfortable. After we had finished, we scattered the crumbs on the grass, and watched the ants appear from nowhere as if by magic to devour them.

'Cute little beggars!' exclaimed Nigel, as one ant attached itself to a crumb twice its size, and proceeded to drag it away backwards to an unknown destination in the grass. 'They've certainly got guts!' He stared straight at me as he said this, and I knew exactly what he was thinking.

'Well, come on!' exclaimed Mariella impatiently, getting up and stretching herself. 'What do we do now?'

'Let's walk along the Wall – the Roman Wall, you know – as far as it goes,' suggested Nigel. 'It's super up there!'

'Isn't it a bit windy?' I put in tentatively.

'Windy?' Nigel squared his shoulders. 'Pooh! That's

nothing! It'll be all the better for that – fewer sightseers about! Come on, Mariella! You can wait for us here, Jane, if you funk it.'

'I don't funk it!' I retorted indignantly. 'I only said it was windy. Surely I can say it's windy if I like.'

'Oh, come on!' repeated Nigel impatiently.

We went out over a stone stile at what had been the North Gate, then walked across a stretch of turf, climbed another stile and found ourselves on top of the Wall. It was quite wide across the top – about six feet, I judged – and the stones were covered with turf, so that it was quite nice to walk on. In front of us was a plantation of Scotch firs and larches, amongst which the wind thundered and roared with the noise of an express train. To the north, the basalt crag on which the Wall was built, fell away sheer, hundreds of feet to the fields far below. The sheep grazing in those far-off pastures looked like toy animals in the vast, rolling landscape.

'Ugh!' I exclaimed, drawing back from the edge with a shudder. 'What a horrid place! It makes my spine creep!'

'Pooh! You're only a silly girl!' scoffed Nigel. 'It's as safe as houses! Look!' He climbed out over the face of an overhanging crag, and sat astride it, laughing. 'Gee up, hoss!'

'Come back, Nigel!' I begged, turning white with fear. 'There might be a landslide, or – or anything!'

'Landslide – not much!' he retorted. 'Why this is genuine British basalt! No landslides here! The jolly old Romans knew where to build their walls, I can tell you! Golly! Fancy making those British johnnies carry these stones by hand all the way up there!' He pointed to the Wall in front of us as it climbed precipitously, like a wicked black snake, to the top of a slope, steep as the roof of a house. 'Gosh! Those were the days!' There was a note of exultation in his voice, and somehow I knew that all his sympathies were with the all-conquering Romans, while mine were all for the poor, down-trodden British.

We climbed up and up until, at the top of the last precipitous slope, the Wall came to an abrupt end – at least, the part you could walk along did, though the Wall itself went snaking along all the way to Carlisle, choosing for itself the highest and rockiest pieces of ground, because they made the best fortification. No obstacle was too difficult for it to surmount!

'Well, this is as far as the National Trust has got,' Nigel told us. 'We'd better turn back now. See those two lakes? Their names are Broomlee and Greenlee. You can't see the biggest one, Crag Lough, from here. It's just round the corner. The best way to get to it is to go along the road nearly as far as that inn called The Twice-brewed, and then turn off to the right across the fields. We'll go there some time – it's a super place – but not today. It's going to rain like billy-ho!'

I felt like saying 'I told you so!' but I didn't. It wasn't really worth the triumph.

We clambered up and down the Wall, skirted a stone enclosure that Nigel told us was a mile-castle, and finally we arrived back at the fir plantation. It was then that I heard it – the faint ba-a-a of a sheep. There was a note of distress in the sound.

'What's that?' I said, stopping in my tracks so suddenly that Nigel, who was coming on behind, nearly fell over me.

'Just a silly sheep,' he answered. 'Do get on, Jane! You're holding up the queue! Surely you've heard a sheep before?'

'Yes, but it sounds different,' I persisted. 'It sounds as if it was lost, or in pain, or something.'

'You're right – it does,' admitted Nigel. 'But anyway, we can't stop now. It's begun to rain.'

'Look!' I said. 'It's down there! ... Oh, poor thing! It must have fallen over, or perhaps it's been blown over.'

Far below us, halfway down the precipitous northern side of the ridge, stuck between a ledge and a clump of straggly nut-trees, was the sheep. It was lying on its back, and struggling feebly. Over our heads, in the darkening sky, floated two sinister back shapes.

'Ravens!' I said with a shudder. "Waiting for it to die!'

'Well, there's nothing we can do about it,' Nigel said definitely.

'But we *must* do something,' I persisted. 'We can't just go away and leave it there. You couldn't – I suppose you couldn't climb down there, Nigel?'

Nigel turned and stared at me.

'What? Me climb down there? Not jolly likely! My good girl, no one but a fly could climb down there.'

'Well, *I'm* going to,' I said, making up my mind in a flash. 'I'm going to have a shot at it anyway.'

'Oh, no you're not!' exclaimed Nigel even more definitely. 'Don't be an idiot, Jane! It'll get right side up again most likely, and climb back by itself.'

'You know it won't! Oh, you *know* it won't!' I yelled, trying to shake off his detaining hand. 'You know very well that when sheep get on their backs, they can't turn over – even just in an ordinary field. You know they've got weak hearts, and after they've struggled a bit, they just die. Everybody knows about "cast" sheep.' Tears

70

filled my eyes. 'And even if it *did* manage to get right way up, it would most probably fall off the ledge while doing it.' With a shudder I looked down where, far below, the jagged rocks stuck out of the sheep-nibbled turf like raisins in a rock cake. 'We *must* do something!'

'Well, we can't risk our lives just for an old sheep,' pronounced Nigel. 'I'm not going to do it myself, and I'm certainly not going to let you, Jane. I'm the man of this party, and *I* shall get all the blame if anything happens to one of you girls. Oh, no you don't!' He held me back by the arms as I rushed forward.

I knew it was useless to argue, and I knew also that I was no match for Nigel – physically, anyway. It would have to be done by subterfuge, if it was done at all.

'All right,' I said sadly. 'I suppose you know best, Nigel. It seems awful though.'

'Yes – it's tough luck,' agreed Nigel. '*I* know! We'll tell that old shepherd chap we saw as we came in – the caretaker johnny. He may be able to think of something.'

'Yes,' I said quietly, knowing in my heart – as I felt sure Nigel did also – that the shepherd would be too late, if indeed we ever found him. The sheep would have struggled and fallen to its doom, or died, long before he got to it.

We made our way back towards the camp. The wind was behind us this time, and it blew us along. We had to lean back on it, so as not to lose our footing! Mariella wanted some of the wild thyme which grows in profusion in the cracks of the Wall, so Nigel took out his pocket-knife to get it for her.

I seized my opportunity.

I doubled back towards the fir wood, fighting my way against the screaming wind. Down the cliff face I climbed, sheer desperation making me brave. Resolutely I pushed the thought of that hideous drop below me to the back of my mind, and merely thought of the poor, helpless sheep on its ledge. Down I went, clinging to bushes and outcrops of rock. Sometimes I hung on by clumps of bracken, while my feet felt for a foothold. Far above me I could hear the frightened screams of Nigel and Mariella, their cries thrown about by the howling wind. Sometimes they reached me clearly – Mariella's shrill: 'Oh, Jane! Please, *please* come back!' and Nigel's deeper, outraged tones: 'Jane, you little idiot! Come back this very minute!'

'It's all right!' I yelled back. 'I'm here! I've got it!'

I had indeed reached the ledge of rock, and was now sitting firmly in the middle of the clump of bushes, the sheep partly in my lap. I had managed to pull it more or less right way up, and the poor thing was so exhausted that it didn't struggle any more, but just stayed passive, panting heavily. This I felt was a blessing. If it had wriggled, I don't know what I should have done.

'Go and get the man!' I yelled as loudly as I could. But Mariella told me afterwards that Nigel had already gone!

It seemed to me that I sat there for hours, but Mariella said that it was only a very short time. Faced with sheer necessity, Nigel had quickly found help. The shepherd arrived, with another close on his heels, and they both carried lengths of stout rope. Our friend, the caretaker, went round to the bottom of the precipice – he knew a path that ordinary people didn't – and climbed up to the ledge, whilst the other man stood at the top and lowered the rope, which he had tied firmly round the trunk of a fir tree, down to me. Between us, the shepherd and I made a

72

sort of cradle for the sheep, and it was hauled to the top, where it scampered off, bleating feebly, then it was my turn. The rope was tied round my waist, and I climbed up by myself. It wasn't nearly so hair-raising as it had been coming down, because I knew that the rope would hold me if I slipped. Finally Jock, our new friend, was pulled up after me.

'Well, ye're a rare plucked 'un, and no mistake!' he said, when we were all safe and sound. 'Mind ye – I'm no saying it wasna a wicked and foolhardy thing for a bit bairn tae dee, but I'll no deny it – ye're a well-plucked young 'un!'

Nigel said nothing, but when we had mounted our ponies, and were riding back towards the gate leading out on to the road, he reined in Max close to me, and surprised me by saying fervently: 'I say, Jane – I'm sorry I said you were a funk just now! I think you're the bravest girl I've ever met – honest injin, I do! You were scared to death of that place – I know you were, yet you climbed down after that silly sheep. Well, if that isn't brave, I don't know what is!'

'Thank you, Nigel,' I said when I'd recovered my breath from shock. 'But I wasn't brave, really. As a matter of fact I never thought of the danger till it was over.'

'Well, having said that,' went on Nigel, 'I'll say something else. If I wasn't on horseback, I'd put you across my knee and spank you, Jane Foster! Of all the little—'

But I knew that he was half joking, and that for the first time in his life, Nigel really admired me!

Chapter 9

I Make a Resolution

MARIELLA and Aunt Irma stayed with us for a whole month, and at the end of that time, Mariella was riding to the manner born. She had very soon decided that Dapple was much too stolid for her, and begged to be allowed to ride Firefly. The result was that I usually rode Dapple, greatly to my relief, whilst Mariella wrestled with my highly-bred birthday present. She didn't seem to mind a bit being thrown off into the ditch.

'I never really hurt myself,' she told me cheerfully as she picked herself up. 'I expect it's being a dancer – you learn to relax. In the ballet, *Job*, Satan has to fall backwards down a flight of steps. Well, he does it again and again, and never hurts himself. It's the same with riding – if you just let yourself go when you fall off, you're quite OK.'

'U-um,' I said doubtfully. It didn't seem to work that way with me!

As a matter of fact, though, Firefly behaved wonderfully well, once he got used to Mariella. We often rode on the moors above Monks Hollow – Mariella seemed to like riding there better than anywhere else.

'It's so high,' she would explain, letting Firefly's reins hang loose on his neck, and stretching her arms above her head in an unconsciously graceful gesture. I couldn't help noticing that every movement she made was graceful. 'And so free – no walls, or fences shutting you in. I'd like to live up here always. Look! Can you see that little cottage just over the brow of the hill? That's where I'd like to live.'

'That's Sally Carruthers' cottage,' I murmured. 'You wouldn't want to live there if you saw inside! It's so damp the paper won't stay on the walls. Poor old Sally is bent double with rheumatism. It has an earth floor, no water or sanitation, and paraffin lamps, *and* there isn't a road to it – only a rough track. Poor Sally has to hump all her groceries, and her paraffin, and even her coal on her back in the winter, because the track is too soft for a wagon or a cart – let alone a motor-van.'

'Well, I'd like to live there all the same,' insisted Mariella. 'I'd have a horse, and make *him* carry my groceries!'

We had tried to keep Mariella's riding a secret at first, but of course the grown-ups found out after a bit. They didn't make as much fuss as we'd feared. Apart from exhorting Mariella not to take any more risks than necessary, Aunt Irma had merely shrugged her shoulders expressively, and murmured something in French that I couldn't understand. To my secret envy, Mariella murmured something back in the same language with what even *I* realized was a perfect accent, and promised (in English) that she'd be frightfully careful. She wouldn't try jumping hedges just yet, however tempting they looked, or broken-down walls. And no, she wouldn't gallop over the open country except when Nigel was with her. This in reply to Mummy's rather anxious homily on the danger of hidden cloughs and open drains.

'You can't see them until you're right on top of them,' Mummy added. 'So do be careful, Mariella.'

Mariella promised, afterwards adding to me:

'I think Mummy realizes that I simply must do other things beside dance. It's too *narrow* to do nothing except dance.'

Well, the four weeks soon went by, and it was with a shock I realized one morning that Mariella's last day had come. In less than an hour's time, we'd be taking them both in to Newcastle to catch the midday train to London.

I was sorry to lose Mariella. I'd got very fond of her, in spite of her rather bossy manner, and her undoubted 'way' with horses, which had sometimes made me feel a bit inferior. But after all, it *had* saved me an awful lot of trouble not having to ride Firefly, and, to do her justice, Mariella had never tried to boss *me*. Yes, on the whole I'd liked having her to stay with us, and above all, I'd loved watching her practise, and hearing her talk about her classes in London, and the strange ways of her temperamental Maestro.

Ever since the night we'd gone to the ballet, I'd been thinking about *Giselle*, and about the dancing lessons I was going to have to cure my round shoulders, and about a girl called Taglioni that Mariella had told me about – a girl who was almost a cripple till she began to dance, but who'd become a world-famous dancer. All the time I was thinking of these things, I was turning over a tremendous scheme in my mind – a scheme I'd told to no one, not even Daddy.

While we were waiting on the platform for the train to go out, I suddenly felt that I could keep my secret to myself no longer, that I must have someone to share it with. After all, Mariella was going away, and it would be ages and ages before I saw her again, so it didn't really matter if she knew.

76

'Mariella!' I said urgently – fortunately Mummy and Aunt Irma were sitting in the compartment talking, and there was a great deal of noise going on around us – porters wheeling luggage about, steam whistling, doors slamming, and all the usual station sounds. Really, we were quite private. 'Mariella,' I repeated, 'is it too late for me to become a dancer?'

Mariella stared at me critically through the smoke and haze of the gloomy Central Station.

'I've known people start later,' she announced. 'Of course, you're more than a year behind the correct age, which is ten, or even nine, but you're awfully young for your age, Jane. If you work hard, who knows? You'll have to manage more than one lesson a week, though. Two, at least, and then three or more, or you'll never do it.'

'Oh, Mariella – you just don't know how much I want to be a dancer,' I whispered.

Mariella looked at me in a funny way.

'Honestly, Jane, I think you're crackers!' she declared. 'Look at what you've got here – a gorgeous place to live in, instead of smelly old London; two ponies all of your own; the Pony Club meetings, and a marvellous cousin like Nigel to teach you to ride. Gosh! How wonderful to be you!'

I looked back at Mariella, and thought of that marvellous place called London which I'd never seen, the Wakulski-Viret studio in Baker Street, Maestro, the funny little Russian dancing master, Covent Garden, parts in the ballets...

'Oh, Mariella,' I said, 'how wonderful to be you!'

The luggage was all in the van by now, and people were standing about, looking expectantly at the guard with his little green flag. A few last-minute passengers came hurrying past, very flustered and out-of-breath.

'I've got a present for you, Mariella,' I said suddenly, looking round anxiously to see that Mummy wasn't listening. 'Something to remember me by.' I thrust a book into Mariella's hands – the book Mummy had given me that day we'd come to the station to meet my cousin and Aunt Irma. 'It will do to read on the train.'

Mariella stared lovingly at the picture of Wendy and her high-stepping steed, and her green eyes grew soft and misty.

'Oh, Jane – how *sweet* of you!' she exclaimed. 'You simply can't imagine how much I wanted it. When you think of poor Wendy, and all the things she went through to get her pony, and then how she nearly wasn't able to ride him in the gymkhana, but managed it after all – gosh! I think it's a perfectly *wonderful* story, don't you?'

I didn't answer because I thought, myself, that it was a terribly silly story, but I didn't want to say so to Mariella because it might have hurt her feelings.

Porters began to bang doors. Mummy dashed out of Aunt Irma's first-class compartment, and the train began to move.

'Mariella!' I yelled, running along the platform in a vain effort to keep pace with my cousin's retreating face at the window, 'I won't say "goodbye", Mariella, because I'll see you in London soon. I'll get there somehow! *Au revoir*, Mariella!'

Chapter 10

Letters

OF course we had both promised to write to each other, so about a week later I wrote to Mariella, and this is what I said.

> Monks Hollow,
> Nr Bychester,
> Northumberland.

Dear Mariella,

I had my first dancing lesson last Friday with the Miss Martin Aunt Irma told Daddy about, and it was *wonderful*! The class was in the evening – after school. It was held in a huge studio with a chandelier in the middle, and lights all round the walls reflecting in the mirrors – just like fairyland. Daddy took me, because Mummy said that dancing wasn't in her line. Daddy seemed to know quite a lot about ballet – I expect it's with being Aunt Irma's, I mean your Mummy's, brother.

Miss Martin isn't temperamental, like your Maestro. At least, if she is she doesn't show it at her classes. She's dark, and very graceful when she moves, and she uses her hands to express herself. She's very kind and gentle, and doesn't shout at you when you do anything wrong, but comes over to you and explains. Not as exciting as your little Maestro, perhaps, but I think I like it better just now!

Well, as I say, the class was wonderful. It wasn't so much the things we did – they were only easy exercises like *pliés*, *grand-battements*, and *ports-de-bras* – but what you might call the 'atmosphere' of the class. You felt you were really on your way to becoming a dancer, like Margot Fonteyn and the Veronica Weston you told me about.

Miss Martin says it will be quite a long time before I do point-work and *fouettés* and things like you, because it's all wrong to hurry these things, and you must get strength first, but she was awfully interested when I told her about you and Aunt Irma, and about how much I wanted to dance.

I was much the biggest in the class – most of them were quite young children – but Miss Martin wasn't at all gloomy about my age. She says you often get on even better when you're old – from ten to twelve – especially if it's really *you* who wants to dance, and not some grown-up pushing you from behind.

I'm going to work for some RAD exams – that's short for Royal Academy of Dancing, but of course you know that. Miss Martin says it's good for your technique to work for exams, though it isn't good to think *only* about exams as some people do. You mustn't be what Mummy calls a 'pot-hunter'. That's a person who goes round to all the gymkhanas collecting silver cups, instead of riding for the joy of it. Personally, I can't imagine anyone going to a gymkhana for the joy of it, but perhaps you can understand Mummy's point of view!

Well, to get back to the dancing – you've got to 'group' your fingers in such a funny way until you've passed the Elementary examination. If you're not

80

frightfully careful, your hand looks just like a duck's bill! Miss Martin says it's to stop you from doing all sorts of funny things with your fingers, and getting affected hands like a lot of dancers have.

I'm practising every day up in the south attic, where you used to dance, remember? I'm trying hard to do all the things you and Miss Martin told me – turning out from the hips, and stretching my feet; and, of course, grouping my fingers. After a discreet interval, I'm going to ask Daddy about the two lessons a week. I feel that Daddy will understand more than Mummy.

Oh, most important! Will you please thank Aunt Irma tremendously for the glorious pair of pink satin *demie-pointe* shoes, and also the lovely broad satin ribbon to put on them. I backed the ribbons with tape where they join on to the shoes, as you showed me. Miss Martin was most approving. She says they will give me no end of support because they're so broad! I do think it was perfectly *sweet* of Aunt Irma to send them, and also to promise to give me my first pair of point shoes. Alas! I feel that's a long way off!

This is an awfully long letter, but I felt I just *had* to tell someone about it – I mean about my dancing.

Lots of love to you and Aunt Irma and Uncle Oscar.

JANE

PS – Nigel did awfully well at the Pony Club gymkhana as usual. He won the Mile Over Fences, and several other events – I can't remember which – and he came in second for Musical Stalls, and the Bending, and something else, I think, but I forget what it was. I'm afraid I disgraced myself. I came in last for nearly everything. Firefly 'ran out' for the Under 14 Jumping, and I came off. Luckily I didn't break anything – I mean it was lucky for my dancing. I was frightfully stiff afterwards, though, and doing *grand-battements* was *agony*. I've got over it now. Nigel said he wished you were there; he thought you'd have managed better than me!

Love again,

JANE

After a week or two, I heard from Mariella. She wrote as follows.

140a Fortnum Mansions,
London, W1.

Dear Jane,

Thank you most awfully for your letter. I was thrilled to hear all about Nigel and the gymkhana. Yes, of course, I knew he'd do well – he's such a marvellous rider. I was very sorry to hear that you didn't have any luck yourself. I expect you haven't quite got used to Firefly yet. Nigel says he's a bit nervous, being highly bred, but he'll be all the more fun to ride when you get the hang of him. Nobody wants to ride a rocking-horse! Have you tried having an impromptu gymkhana in your paddock? That would get him used to the jumps and hurdles and things. Nigel and I were talking about it just before I came back to London, and he knew several people who he was sure would want to come. That would get Firefly used to having strange ponies about. I think it's a wonderful idea of Nigel's, don't you?

Is Firefly getting any better at opening gates? Have you tried persuading someone to stand on the far side of the gate with a carrot? I'm pretty sure if Firefly found out that a gate meant a carrot, he'd stop being frightened of them. He's awfully greedy, and a proper donkey when it comes to carrots!

I'm getting quite a library of pony books. It was most awfully sweet of you to give me your new Wendy book as a goodbye present. I don't know how you could bear to part with it. I've read it quite ten times – not counting the journey home – and I look at the cover every night before I go to sleep in the hopes that I'll dream about Monks Hollow, and Firefly, and everything. I am sending you a book of mine in exchange. It's called *First Steps*, and it's by two famous people, Ruth French, who was *première danseuse* in Pavlova's company, and Felix Demery. Mummy says this is the book you'll need if you're going to work for the RAD exams. I haven't read it myself – it looks pretty dull, but I expect Mummy's right, and it'll be ever so useful!

I've discovered a leather shop near Covent Garden that sells things for horses, and I've got quite a lot of grooming kit, and a hoof-pick, and a riding-crop. They're not much use to me here except to look at, but I thought they'd come in useful when I stay with you next time. Mummy says it's your turn to come and stay with us in London, but as I pointed out to her that would be frightfully dull for you. What on earth should we do to entertain you? *We* haven't got a lovely garden, or fields, or two ponies, or miles and miles of glorious moorland, like you in Northumberland. We've only got shops, and streets, and theatres, and nobody in their right mind wants to see *them*. Perhaps I could come to stay with you, as well as you coming here –

that is if you really *want* to come here, but I shouldn't, if I were you!

This letter is nearly as long as yours! It's nice to have someone to talk to about the Things that Matter. Here, they're always talking 'shop' – all about the latest ballet they're doing in the Company, and the choreography, and how awful the décor and the costumes are, and how Delia McFarlane is going to be better than Belinda Beaucaire after all, and so on. You've no idea how boring it gets!

Lots of love,

MARIELLA

PS – I'm so glad your dancing lesson turned out all right. Wait till you've been at it a couple of years! You'll be wiser then!

After I had read the letter, I took it up to my bedroom and read it all through again – at least, I read the last part. Not that there was much in it about dancing, but even to read Mariella's writing seemed to bring London and the ballet nearer.

Finally, I put the letter away in a drawer, and went over to the window. My room faced north, and there, before me, stretched Northumberland. Miles and miles of misty, purple moorland; miles and miles of sheep-nibbled turf covering the huge, rounded hills; miles and miles of trackless fir woods, stretching up and up to the Border. It was all so spacious, it made me feel very small and insignificant. It was also beautiful and wild, and I felt this now, as I had never done before. Yet I deliberately turned my back upon it, and faced towards the south, where London was.

'I'm going to dance!' I said to myself, shutting my eyes tightly, and trying to imagine myself in Mariella's studio in Baker Street. 'I'm not going to be a kennel-maid, or look after somebody's horses; I'm not going to be a veterinary surgeon. I'm going to be a dancer!'

Part Two

I Go to London
Written by Jane

Chapter 1

Journey South

I'M afraid that neither Mariella nor I were very good at writing letters. Apart from the two long ones we had written to each other during the first two weeks of our separation, our correspondence was limited to Christmas and birthday cards. Two years passed before I had a letter from her again, though Aunt Irma had kept her promise, and had sent me my first pair of blocked ballet shoes. Beautiful shoes they were, too, with the usual length of pink satin ribbon to sew on them.

Of course, I dare say Mariella had been busy all this time. I know *I* had! Besides my school work, I'd managed to increase my dancing lessons to three a week, and now, more often than not, I had four – one on Saturday morning as well! Mummy simply couldn't understand why I insisted upon getting up at seven o'clock every Saturday morning – Saturday was a day when Daddy didn't go in to the office by car – to catch the eight o'clock bus into town, but fortunately she didn't forbid me to do it. It was very pleasant in the summer-time, with the mist lifting off the moors, and the curlews calling, and the larks singing their heads off in the blue air, but in the depths of winter, it was frankly a nightmare! As I let myself out of the house into the cold Northumbrian morning, and waited in the half-dark for the bus, I cheered myself with thoughts of London and Mariella. The bus came from another village, farther up in the hills, and more often than not it had icicles hanging round its sides, and a thick blanket of snow on its roof.

At the end of a year, I took my first RAD Children's examination. As a matter of fact I took Grades Four and Five together because Miss Martin didn't insist upon my taking all the first Grades. I passed with Honours, and after this I began working for my first senior exam, the Elementary. Miss Martin told me that quite a different standard of work was required for this exam from that expected for the Children's Grades, and that I should have to work hard for it.

For the Children's Grades, I wore a white silk frock with a circular skirt and a low-cut neckline, and knickers to match. I had white socks and unblocked ballet shoes. For my Elementary, which I took in Edinburgh, I wore a real *tutu*. A *tutu* is a ballet dress made of stiff tarlatan. The bodice is of satin, tightly fitted, and ending at the waistline. Then another piece of satin is joined on to the bodice and comes down to the hips. After this comes the stiff, frilled skirt with frilly trunks – made all in a piece with the dress. The effect is lovely – like the corolla of a flower. But the idea of wearing a classical *tutu* for exams isn't only because it looks lovely. One reason for the rule is that it's the traditional classical costume, and as I expect you know, there's an awful lot of tradition in ballet. The second reason is that the dress shows exactly what

I wore a real tutu

you're doing. No hope of hiding bad dancing in a *tutu*. Incidentally I wore pink tights with my *tutu*, and a piece of pink net round my hair to keep it tidy.

I took my Elementary exam nine months after I'd taken my Children's Grades, and I got eighty for it, which Miss Martin said was 'very satisfactory'. You mustn't imagine that we thought of nothing but exams at Miss Martin's classes. Far from it! We did all kinds of dancing, besides RAD – Greek, and Character, and quite a lot of Checcetti, which is named after the famous Italian dancing master. We also had a class which Miss Martin called 'Sadler's Wells'. In it she told us about Ninette de Valois' new syllabus, which is different from anybody else's, and we did a lot of the exercises. Ninette de Valois is the director of the Sadler's Wells Ballet, of course. I'm saying 'of course', which is really very funny, because only two years ago I'd never heard of Ninette de Valois, myself. I hadn't even heard of Pavlova or Margot Fonteyn! I learnt one frightfully interesting thing, and that was that the great dancer, Veronica Weston, once went to Miss Martin's classes for a whole year! Imagine doing *pliés* at the very same *barre* where Veronica Weston did them!

It was at the beginning of August – just about two years after Mariella and Aunt Irma had stayed with us – that I heard from my cousin again. She wrote:

> 140a Fortnum Mansions,
> London, W1.

Dear Jane,

I expect you are thinking awful things about me for not having written to you all this time. I have no excuse except the usual one – too busy! And that's no excuse, really, because everyone knows you can always find time to do what you want to do, no matter how busy you are. The truth is I just *hate* writing letters! I've thought about you lots, though. Every time I see a horse in the Row, I think about you, and Nigel, and Firefly, and wonder how you are getting along.

Everything is much as usual here. I still go to Madame's classes, and Maestro is just as funny. I expect I shall be leaving soon, though, because I'm nearly fifteen, and I'm going to the Sadler's Wells Ballet School. At least, I am if they'll have me! My audition is in ten days' time. I'm not looking forward to it much, I can tell you!

Now comes the important point of this letter. Can you come and stay with me for a week or two? Mummy has just gone on a tour to New Zealand to give a series of lectures on ballet, so there's only Daddy and me here. Daddy is so absent-minded he forgets about me for days on end, so it's almost the same as having nobody at all, and I'm dreadfully lonely. Do say you'll come, Jane! How about next week? All you need do is send a wire, and I'll meet you at the station.

Lots of love,

MARIELLA

When I'd read the letter, I passed it over to Mummy who was pouring out the breakfast coffee. She hummed and ha'ed, and began talking about all the new clothes I'd need if I went to London. I couldn't possibly go walking down Regent Street, she said, in an ancient pair of jodhpurs and a washed-out blouse, as I did here. I'd have to have a new coat, and a couple of frocks to go with it, not to mention shoes, and a hat for Sunday.

'Well, why not?' broke in Daddy. 'Jane is fourteen now. She's beginning to take an interest in her clothes, aren't you, Jane? Why not take her to one of those big Newcastle shops that have special departments for people Jane's age, and fit her out. Or, if you can't be bothered, let Irma do it at Harrods. If I know Irma, there's nothing she would like better.'

'You forget,' said Mummy patiently, 'that Irma is on the high seas.'

'So she is!' laughed Daddy. 'Well, you'll just have to do it yourself, then.'

The upshot of the matter was that at precisely ten-thirty on the night of August 10th, I found myself being ushered into a sleeper on the Newcastle to King's Cross express. After a lot of arguments, Mummy and Daddy had decided that, if I was shut into a first-class sleeper, and put in charge of the sleeping-car attendant, I couldn't really come to much harm. I had strict injunctions to stay in my compartment until eight o'clock (the train arrived at a much earlier hour, but you were allowed to stay in it), when I was to issue forth with a porter who would be found for me by the obliging sleeping-car attendant. The porter would have instructions to stay with me until I was safely with my friends.

When the train began to move, and Mummy and Daddy's anxious faces had disappeared from outside the corridor window, I went back into my sleeper. It was just like an ordinary bedroom, with its washbasin, and proper little bed against the wall. There were ever so many electric lights which I switched on, one after the other, and a heating device which didn't work because I tried it. Probably that was because it was the middle of August, and the railway company didn't think you needed any heat during the summer.

It seemed awfully strange to get undressed in a swaying, creaking train, and even stranger to clean your teeth in it! After I had done these things, I brushed my hair, and smoothed it down very sleekly with my fingers on either side of my centre parting, hoping I looked a teeny bit like Alicia Markova, or Margot Fonteyn! I was very glad I was pale-faced, though I must say it was strange that Mariella, living in London, should be as rosy as a piece of apple blossom, whilst I, who had lived all my life in the depths of the country, should be as pale as skimmed milk. This last was Nigel's description of my complexion, and I don't think it was very kind of him to say it, because everyone knows that skimmed milk is a horrid blue colour, and my skin wasn't a bit like that, really.

I lay down in my comfortable bed, and tried to go to sleep. The faint blue light on the ceiling swayed and danced with the movements of the train, as it sped swiftly through the night like a fairy dragon, bearing me towards that great and mysterious city of London. London, my goal! I couldn't help being terribly excited at the mere thought of it, even though I was only going there for a holiday, and not setting out to make my fortune, like Dick Whittington. I tried hard to forget that in five weeks' time I'd be back again on this very train – only going the other way! In after-years I couldn't help thinking how much more excited I'd have been if I had known all the things that were going to happen to me during those five weeks; how my entire life was going to be changed.

As it was I lay there, thinking how lucky Mariella was to live in London, cheek-by-jowl with Covent Garden, and all the famous dancing schools, and how awful it was to be me, and to have to go on exercising Firefly and Dapple day in, day out, and trying to take an interest in the Pony Club gymkhana.

Outside my compartment, the train seemed to be full of noise and bustle. People kept opening and shutting doors, and laughing. Sometimes they bumped against my door, as the train swayed round corners. Once, the ticket collector came in and demanded my ticket, and asked me what time I wanted my tea in the morning.

'As late as possible!' I laughed.

'Seven-thirty it is, miss,' he said. 'That's as late as I can make it. Goodnight, miss, and pleasant dreams!'

I didn't know whether to wish *him* pleasant dreams back, because I supposed he'd spend most of the night collecting tickets, and looking after people generally.

After this, nothing happened for quite a long time, and I was nearly asleep, when suddenly my door flew open, and a person clad in a bright green dressing-gown and curling-pins switched on the light, and then nearly fell on top of me, as the train gave a sudden lurch.

'S-sorry!' she apologized. 'Wrong compartment! I *am* so sorry!' So saying, she disappeared as suddenly as she had come, switching the light off as she went. I decided that it might be wise to bolt my door, so I got up and did so.

Then I think I must have gone to sleep, for the next thing I remember was a grinding of brakes, together with an awful clattering, rattling noise, shouts of porters, supercilious drawl of loudspeakers, bustle, and hurry generally. I peeped behind my blind, and saw that we were standing in a big, dark station. Quite a lot of people were getting off the train, looking half asleep, whilst

94

others were boarding it. Then I saw, round the top of a lamp, the words Y-O-R-K, so I knew that that was the name of the station.

We didn't stay long in York. Soon we were off again on our long journey south. The train was very silent now. Except for the grinding whirr of the wheels, and the squeaking of the couplings there wasn't another sound. I couldn't help thinking about the engine driver and the guard, holding in their hands the lives of all those hundreds of trustful, sleeping people. I must have slept again myself very soon, for the next time I woke, we were just gliding gently into another station. It was a very long, dark station, and with a leaping at my heart, I saw its name K-I-N-G-'S C-R-O-S-S on a large board on the platform as we slid past.

I looked at my wristwatch. It was still very early – hours yet before I could leave the train – so I cuddled down again underneath my bedclothes, telling myself firmly that I must go to sleep. Alas, I couldn't! It was altogether too thrilling to be really in London at last – London, the city of my dreams!

Chapter 2

London at Last!

AT half past seven my tea arrived, and at eight o'clock precisely the sleeping-car attendant appeared with a porter in tow. The latter collected my luggage, perched it on a trolly together with mountains of other baggage, and wheeled it away. I followed on behind, feeling very small and rather lonely.

Mariella met me as she had promised. I saw her waving frantically while I was still quite a long way off the barrier. She was dressed in green linen, and she wore no hat over her bright curls. I thought she looked prettier than ever. Standing just behind her was a quiet-looking little man that I knew must be Uncle Oscar whom I had never met. I had learnt quite a lot about him, though, from Mummy and Daddy, and from Mariella, herself. Uncle Oscar was always referred to as 'Irma Foster's husband'. He was what is known as a 'critic'.

'Oh, Daddy does everything second-hand,' Mariella explained rather cruelly I thought at the time. 'He knows everything there is to know about ballet, music, and art, though he's never danced a step, played a note, or held a paintbrush in his fingers! He just pulls the work of other people to pieces, without having the bother of learning to do it himself. Perhaps if he had to do it himself he wouldn't be so critical!'

As for Uncle Oscar's appearance – well, the first thing I saw was that he wasn't the least bit like Mariella. He was more like me, being small and pale, with rather sad, dark eyes. He was bald, too, and he wore a small, drooping moustache that somehow matched his eyes. He spoke gently, and seemed very kind. Really, it was hard to believe that he could 'pull people to pieces' as Mariella declared he did when he was criticizing their work. It was evident that he was also very absent-minded, and if it hadn't been for my porter, we'd most certainly have bowled off in the taxi without any of my luggage!

No 140a Fortnum Mansions was in a huge block of flats looking out over Regent's Park. The Fosters lived on the fourth floor, and you went up in a lift. It was lovely when you got there – I mean on the fourth floor. The air was quite clear and sunny – not a bit dark and foggy as I had always imagined it to be in London.

Mariella took me straight to her bedroom, which had two beds in it and french windows leading out on to a little wrought-iron balcony. There was a garden-seat with gay cushions on it on the balcony, and a window-box full of geraniums and lobelia, and a flowering tree in a green-painted tub. By the side of the balcony was the fire-escape, zigzagging down to the ground. It was really very quiet in Mariella's bedroom. Apart from the faint roar of traffic in the distance and the occasional whine of a car changing gear on the road far below, you could almost have imagined you were in the country. You could even hear the twittering of birds, though they *were* only common or garden sparrows, and not thrushes and blackbirds, as Mariella was careful to point out.

'I think this is a perfectly lovely place,' I declared, looking round at the softly carpeted room, with its long mirrors and soft cushions.

'Wait till you've lived here for a bit,' said Mariella,

throwing her coat on to her bed. 'Then you'll appreciate the real country. Why, even the very name of this place' – Mariella made a little *moue* of disgust with her mouth – 'one-four-o(a) Fortnum Mansions, makes you feel like a convict, or a private in the Army, or something! Think of the lovely names of the places where you live – Corbirigg – Meadowsley – Dewburn – Bracken Hall – Up-and-Down Cottage. Think of your own home, Monks Hollow. Think of it at this very moment. The ring-doves will be coming in the little copse outside your bedroom window, Jane.'

I laughed.

'All I can think of at the moment is that Covent Garden is just round the corner, and your Maestro's studio only a stone's throw away!'

'You're still keen on dancing, then?' questioned Mariella, running a comb through her bright curls.

'Frightfully.'

'Well, we can do a bit of practising together, then,' she laughed. 'Officially speaking, I'm supposed to be on holiday, but I still have to practise because of my beastly audition. The worst of it is, I'm so horribly lazy.' She stretched her arms above her head in a graceful gesture and yawned. 'The mere idea of *pliés* and *grands-battements* makes me feel tired! As a matter of fact, though, quite a lot of us at Madame's are in the same boat for one reason or another, so Maestro is going on with the classes all through the hols. Madame, herself, has sheered off to Nice, or Cannes, or somewhere, but I really believe that Maestro was quite *glad* of an excuse to go on with his old classes! So you're lucky, Jane. You'll see the mighty man! There's a practice-room at Madame's, and I go there every morning from ten o'clock till twelve. You can come with me if you like.'

'Oh, *thank* you!' I said fervently. 'I'd simply adore to.'

Mariella stared at me thoughtfully for a moment or two without speaking. Then she burst out:

'You *are* funny, Jane! I really believe you *like* practising!'

Before I had time to answer, she opened the door and bustled me out into the little square hall of the flat. I couldn't help feeling how funny it was to have a hall up on the fourth floor! Opening out of the hall were all the other rooms of the flat – six of them; Mariella told me.

'It must seem terribly queer and small to you, Jane,' she declared. 'Why, I should think there are quite six storerooms at Monks Hollow, let alone all the rest of the house! Well, this is our lounge.' She led me into a long room that obviously did duty both as sitting-room and dining-room – the latter being at one end, and the lounge at the other. There were sliding doors between the two rooms, but they stood open now.

'We shut them in the winter,' Mariella told me, 'to make it more cosy.'

Breakfast came up through the floor on a sort of lift as if by magic, though, as a matter of fact, it was supplied by the restaurant on the ground floor as Mariella explained when she saw my amazed expression. 'You order it through the speaking-tube, and, hey presto! it appears – sooner or later! More often the latter! Porridge, Jane?'

The porridge wasn't a bit like the kind we had at home. In fact, I must admit that it was more like that stuff you buy in glass jars to stick labels on with! Mariella didn't have any, because she said it was fattening!

We had breakfast by ourselves because Uncle Oscar had gone out to do some research at the London Library, having totally forgotten that he hadn't yet had his breakfast – at least, Mariella said so! When we had finished our meal, she showed me over the rest of the flat. There wasn't much more to it, since it all opened off the same little vestibule, as I said before. There were a couple of bedrooms, Aunt Irma's sitting-room, and Uncle Oscar's library. Apart from a couple of large bookcases, reaching from floor to ceiling, Uncle Oscar's library was chock-a-block full of glass cabinets, and glass-fronted showcases, and these were full of ornaments and jewellery in jade. Mariella explained that her father was a collector, besides being a critic, and that he'd collected his jade all over the world. It was while he was in China, on the track of some special kind of antique cloak-hooks for his collection, that he'd met Aunt Irma, and collected her instead!

At half past nine, we shut the door of the flat behind us, sped down in the lift, and set off for Baker Street, which Mariella said was quite near, and where Madame's studio was. We each carried a small case with our shoes and tights in it. I felt very important, going to a real London dancing school (even if it *was* only to practise) with the daughter of a world-famous ballerina (even if she *was* my cousin).

The studio was at the Regent's Park end of Baker Street, and on a brass plate at the side of the narrow entrance were the following inscriptions:

1ST FLOOR. WORRIT, SNARK AND SNARK, SOLICITORS, COMMISSIONERS FOR OATHS

2ND FLOOR. MISS SADIE CALLENDER. EMPLOYMENT AGENCY

On the other side of the entrance, was a large plate-
glass window containing one black and gold hat-stand,
with a hat of extremely strange shape upon it, one pair of
long, black suede gloves, a handbag nearly as big as an
attaché-case, and a small white kitten, which yawned
delicately, and stretched itself when we tapped upon the
glass to attract its attention.

'Awful, isn't it?' Mariella remarked. 'I mean the hat, of
course, not Fifi. She's rather a sweet. Somebody frightfully
good-looking might wear it and get away with it – somebody like Mummy, for instance. But, funnily enough, it's
always the other kind who want to wear hats like that.
When I came here to practise a day or two ago, a friend of
Mummy's was trying one on. I saw her when I called for
something they were doing for Mummy. It was a perfectly ghastly hat, worse than this one, though I know
you'd think it couldn't possibly be, and she – Lady Bailey
– is fat and at least fifty or sixty, with goodness knows
how many chins and no neck. She's got oodles of money,
but no taste. Gosh! You should have seen her in that hat,
with the feather tickling her nose, and Madame Jacques
telling her solemnly that it was "just Modom's type –
simply made for Modom!"' Wickedly Mariella mimicked
the manageress of the hat shop. 'Fortunately,' she added,
'it didn't fit, so we were spared the shocking sight
of Lady Bailey in one of Madame Jacques' latest
creations! Well, come on, Jane! Up we go! There's no
lift here!'

We dashed up the three flights of stone stairs, and finally came to a suite of rooms, from one of which came the sound of the tapping of a stick on the floor, the tinkle of a piano, and – most exciting of all! – a foreign voice counting, and issuing commands.

'That's Maestro!' said Mariella. 'He's at it already! In here, Jane.'

I found myself in a small, bare room, lined with mirrors, and with *barres* along the walls. For a moment I was disappointed. It was so much smaller than Miss Martin's practice-room at home, and it obviously did duty for dressing-room as well, for, when I looked round, Mariella was already changing into her dancing things. Then I remembered the foreign voice next door and a thrill of excitement shot through me. I was within speaking distance of Mariella's wonderful Maestro!

Chapter 3

The Baker Street Studio

'I DON'T suppose anyone else will turn up this morning,' Mariella said, as we tied our shoes. 'There's a rehearsal of *Italian Rhapsody* at ten, and most of them are in it. The rest are in there' – she nodded towards the room where the piano was. 'My class isn't till late this afternoon. I expect there will be masses of people at it – all the Rhapsodies will be back by then.'

We began our practice facing the *barre* with exercises for *pliés*. Then we went on to *battements-tendus*, *battements-glissés*, *relevés* in second. Then we did plain *grands-battements* to the back, with both hands on the *barre*. After we had finished at the *barre*, we did some centre-practice – *pirouettes*, and *fouettés*, and things. Then we tried some *enchainements* that Mariella said were favourites with Maestro.

After we had finished, Mariella stood leaning against the *barre*, and stared hard at me.

'Goodness, Jane!' she exclaimed, breathing hard. 'You *are* good! I just can't believe that when I saw you last, you hadn't even started. You aren't as advanced as me, of course, but you do lots of things just as well. In fact, I think your *pirouettes* and *fouettés* are a lot better! Sometimes I feel I've gone down,' she added sadly. 'I have an idea Mummy thinks so too. I believe she knows in her heart that I shall never be a dancer – not a dancer like she was, anyway. I just don't seem to *want* to dance.'

103

'Aren't you even looking forward to your audition for the Sadler's Wells Ballet School?' I asked incredulously.

'Not a bit,' confessed Mariella. 'In fact, quite frankly I loathe the thought of it. Gosh! What a frightfully expressive face you've got, Jane! I can see you think I'm quite batty not to appreciate the honour of an audition for Sadler's Wells. But I don't, so there! I wish you could go instead.'

'Oh, but Mariella – I couldn't!' I gasped.

'No, of course not,' said Mariella, stripping off her practice tights. 'I was only joking. But wouldn't it be fun if you could. Wouldn't it be a joke if *you* got accepted, Jane! I believe you would, whereas I'm pretty sure *I* shan't. Or if I do, it'll only be because of Mummy. Naturally they'll think I'm *bound* to be good, being Irma Foster's daughter!'

'Who's that talking about Irma Foster?' said a voice so close to my ear that I jumped.

'Oh, it's you, Kathleen Mavourneen!' said Mariella. 'Why will you always appear and disappear as silently as Hamlet's ghost? You've scared Jane stiff! She's gone quite white. She's not used to ghosts! By the way, Jane – this is Kathleen O'Shaunessy. She comes from old Ireland, as you might guess from the length of her eyelashes! Kathleen – Jane Foster.'

'Oh, a relation of yours is it?' asked Kathleen in her soft Irish brogue.

'Yes – my cousin.'

'And is it a dancer she's after being, too?'

'Well – she *wants* to be,' Mariella answered. '*Why,* goodness knows! You should just see the perfectly gorgeous place where Jane lives. It's in Northumberland – all among the moors and woods, and they've got the loveliest house. Jane's got two ponies, called Firefly and Dapple, and a terribly attractive cousin, Nigel, who knows everything there is to know about horses. Wouldn't you think she'd stay there, in Northumberland, when she's got all that, instead of hankering after sore toes and rehearsals?'

Kathleen shrugged her shoulders expressively.

'There's no accounting for tastes, but as for meself I'd rather be doing *pas de cheval* on me own feet than perched up on a real horse, so I would!'

'You are funny!' giggled Mariella. 'Really, you ought to be in musical comedy. That show at the Gaiety, *Dance for Poppa*, would jump at you! And you never know – you might shoot to the top in it like Marcia Rutherford. Gosh! What a lot of money that girl must earn! Every time I pass the Gaiety at night, and see:

'M-A-R-C-I-A—R-U-T-H-E-R-F-O-R-D
I-N
D-A-N-C-E – F-O-R – P-O-P-P-A

'in electric lights a mile high, I wonder how much she gets a week. An awful lot more than they ever paid Mummy, I bet! And that show's been running for four years already.'

'Have you met the lady?' asked Kathleen softly.

'No – why?'

'Just because *I have*, that's all,' murmured Kathleen. 'She's the most ghastly girl you could meet in a month of Sundays! But, of course, it's glamour she's got, and pep – call it what you like. Hey, ho!' she stretched herself. 'It's nearly dead I am, after my class! I always said Maestro was after killing me!'

'Where are all the others?' asked Mariella.

105

'Och, they'll be here in a minute,' answered Kathleen. 'They stayed behind to rehearse that *corps de ballet* bit of *Les Sylphides* we're doing at the Charity matinée on Saturday.'

'Let's get away then, Jane, before the stampede of the wild animals!'

As we walked home up Baker Street, Mariella was unusually silent. Suddenly she exclaimed: '*I* know! Why shouldn't you come to one of my classes? – I mean a real class, not just practising.'

'Oh, but I couldn't!' I said. 'Why, I'm a stranger.'

'That doesn't matter,' Mariella assured me. 'Strangers often join in classes – especially during the hols. I can ask Miss Darnley, Madame's secretary, to arrange it, and send the bill in to Daddy. He'll never notice that it isn't for me.'

'Oh, but I *couldn't* do that!' I expostulated. 'Poor Uncle Oscar!'

'Oh, Jane – do stop saying "I couldn't" like that!' Mariella exclaimed in exasperation. 'Daddy's got oodles of money, so you needn't worry. Criticism is very well paid – much better paid than the artists and the people who get criticized are! But if it'll make you feel more comfortable, I'll ask him first. You'd better not come with me this afternoon, though, because you'll be tired after travelling all night, and you don't want to be tired for Maestro's class, I can tell you! You'll be tired enough after it's finished! But I'll be going again tomorrow, and you can join in then.'

'Yes, but what about your Maestro?' I asked anxiously. 'Are you *quite* sure, Mariella, that he won't mind having me gatecrash into his class?'

106

'He might if you weren't so good,' Mariella said candidly. 'But, as it is, I fancy he'll be thrilled to death. You're really most awfully promising, you know, Jane. Honestly, I'd *like* him to see you.'

'Well, I'd give anything to see *him*,' I said with a sigh of delight at the mere thought. 'Even just to *see* him would be worth coming to London!'

Again Mariella stared at me.

'You *are* funny, Jane!' she said as we turned in at the main entrance hall to Fortnum Mansions.

Chapter 4

A Lesson with Maestro

NEXT morning Mariella took me on top of a bus to see some of the things she said she supposed I ought to see while I was in London – Westminster Abbey, the Tower, London Bridge, Marble Arch, and the statue of Eros in Piccadilly Circus. She ended up by taking me up and down the escalator at Leicester Square, which she said was the longest one on the Underground, and then we went home to the flat where we had lunch. We had it by ourselves, as Uncle Oscar was taking the chair at a committee meeting at one of his various literary societies, and was having lunch at his club in Jermyn Street.

'You see how lonely I'd have been if you hadn't come to stay, Jane?' Mariella said as we helped ourselves to salmon mayonnaise from the accommodating lift-table. 'I do wish they'd shred the lettuce in their salads like you had yours when I stayed with you' – she poked a large lettuce leaf disgustedly. 'They just don't know how to make a salad in London.'

'Never mind,' I said, glancing at the dainty sweets in the little glass wishes. 'All the rest of the things are lovely.'

'Um—' Mariella said doubtfully. 'Wait till you've lived on them for a few weeks, then you'll be wiser! They all taste exactly the same. I'd rather have a dish of real fruit out of your garden, with real cream on it, Jane, than all this fancy stuff. You can have my trifle, by the way. I'm not supposed to eat it. I'm getting too fat.'

'I don't think you're fat at all,' I said. 'I think you're just perfect,' and indeed, as she stood by the window of the lounge, with a ray of sunshine falling across her bright hair, her green eyes dancing, she looked the picture of beauty and grace.

'Thank you,' Mariella said simply. 'Of course I know I'm not fat according to ordinary standards, but for ballet you've got to be really slim – like you are. And there's no getting away from the fact – I'm no fairy! Gosh! That reminds me – when I was stretching yesterday I split my tights. I must rush and darn them before clsss. That's the worst of being fat!'

She dashed away, and I ate both the trifles with slow delight. I thought they were lovely, even if the cream on them wasn't real. In fact I thought everything was lovely – even the noise and bustle of London, and the great blocks of buildings closing you in on every side. All new to me, and terribly exciting. Lucky, lucky Mariella, I thought, to live here always!...

We walked to the studio again because of Mariella's thighs. Anyway, as I said before, it was a very short distance.

The hat was still perched upon its ornate pedestal in solitary splendour. The white kitten was still asleep on its cushion; the piano, when we got to the third floor, still tinkled from behind the closed door of the main studio.

'That's the boys' class,' explained Mariella. 'Let's hope they're in good form, then he'll be in a decent temper!'

The little practice-cum-dressing-room was crowded with girls of all ages and sizes. Mariella said afterwards that there were only fourteen, but there seemed hundreds to me! They didn't seem to mind my gatecrashing in amongst them a bit, in fact they were all very helpful. One of them – a girl called Julia – showed me exactly how Maestro liked you to do your hair – in plaits on top of your head, with a piece of net over it. As I hadn't any net, someone else lent me a bit.

As we waited for the boys' class to finish, most of us passed the time by doing stretching exercises on the *barres*, or *pliés*. Mariella stood by the door gossiping with two of her special friends – a girl called Anna, who spoke with a foreign accent, and another called Chloë, who had a most wonderful complexion like peaches and cream, enormous dark eyes, and sweeping eyelashes. I couldn't help staring at her and thinking how lovely she was – like a vivid, glowing flower.

At last there was a mild commotion next door, the piano became silent, and a stream of boys, dressed in black tights and short-sleeved white shirts, emerged. They were all talking at once, and it seemed to me that they were all doing it in different languages! Mariella told me afterwards that there were only six or seven.

'Come on!' said the lovely Chloë. 'What are we waiting for? Let's hope he'll be in a good temper! ... Anna! Your hair was perfect before. Why on earth must you start doing it all over again *now*? He'll be livid if you're late for the third day running!'

Anna merely shrugged her shoulders, and went on imperturbably plaiting her dark hair. The rest of us filed into the now empty studio. It was a large, bare room, with three windows high up in the wall on one side, and of course the usual mirrors and *barres*. At the far end there was a low rostrum, and on it, deep in conversation with the pianist, stood a slight figure in flannel slacks and open-necked shirt. A thrill of excitement shot through me — I was in the presence of Mariella's little Maestro — the Russian dancing master she'd told me about so long ago.

He was slim, lithe, and, though not very tall, he moved with a graceful stride that somehow reminded me of a wild animal, though he wasn't at all wild to look at himself. He had aquiline features — high-bridged nose, with thin, sensitive nostrils; thin-lipped, mobile mouth; glittering dark eyes, and thick, black hair, cut very short. His feet were small; his hands thin and nervous. All these things might seem ordinary enough, but put together they made up a personality anything but ordinary. Maestro, the Russian, was dynamic. Everything about him was expressive — from his small, rubber-shod feet, to his very eyebrows, one cocked higher than the other. Vitality issued from him, like sparks from a cat's fur, and all this vitality was centred in one thing — the perfection of the Art for which he lived. He was a devotee, a fanatic. He lived for one thing only — Ballet. As for the girls, standing quietly along the *barres* round the room, awaiting his orders — he didn't see them as girls at all, though most of them were beautiful, and he was quite young, himself. To him they were just material, good, bad, and indifferent — mostly indifferent, according to his view — to be made into instruments for his beloved Art.

He swept the lines with a glittering eye:

'Where is Anna?' (He pronounced it 'Ar-nar'.)

'In the dressing-room, Maestro,' one of the girls volunteered. 'She's nearly ready.'

There was an ominous pause; then the explosion.

'In ze dressing-room! In ze *dressing-room*!' stormed the little man. 'What then does she in ze dressing-room at five minutes past ze hour — tell me zat — vile I sit here like

111

ze monument vereon is Patience, and can do nozzing, nozzing whatever, wizout An-na, my pupil ze most advanced? *You*' – he had picked up a little red stick from the table, and now he pointed it at me – 'go you and tell her, please, I wait no longer. Tell her zat as she finds ze dressing-room of more importance zan ze classroom, in ze dressing-room she shall remain . . .'

Fortunately, just at this moment, the tardy Anna arrived, all apologies and charm, the Maestro smiled, and peace was restored. It goes without saying that Anna was his favourite pupil. She aggravated him beyond words, she drove him nearly to madness, as he told her every day, but always she charmed him.

To my surprise, after the first few minutes, the little Russian took quite a lot of notice of me. Several times he said things to me in his odd, broken English, and once he stopped beside me for a long time, watching my every movement. Then he tapped my foot lightly with his stick:

'*En dehors*, leetle one!' Then, as I looked rather mystified, he translated: 'Eet must go round farther, *liebchen* – screw 'im round, so! Yes, but do not make ze sickle-foot. Eet must be *so*.' He took my foot in his hand, and placed it correctly. 'And ze shoulders, *so*. Do not drop ze elbow. Zat ees a nice line you have there. *Jal Ja-ja-ja!* Remember that position.'

It was wonderful. I found I could do the exercise the way he said, and I knew it was right. It *felt* right. The music made me think of the woods at home. I saw in my imagination the sunlight filtering through the branches, and falling in golden pools on the moss-grown path. Strange that there in the heart of London, in this austere, mirror-lined studio, I thought of it, whereas at home I had merely taken it for granted! I'm afraid I forgot all the things the Maestro had told me; I just did the exercise, and tried to express my thoughts in my dancing.

Suddenly, to my horror, the little man stalked majestically back to my end of the room, and stood watching me silently with glittering eyes. I went cold all over. Gosh! What were all those things he'd told me to do? Frantically I tried to remember them ... turn out from the thighs, keep the shoulders down; the elbows up; do not drop the hand ... the ankle ...

'*Stop!*' His stick banged fiercely on the *barre* beside me. '*Stop*, all of you!' He waved to the class in lordly manner; then turned back to me ... 'What do you mean by doing *so* and *so*' – imitation – 'like a duck, or a common farmyard fowl?' – imitation. 'When I do not regard you – or you theenk I do not – you do eet *so*! – *beau-ti-fully*. Even I, Ivan Dmitoritch Stcherbakof, would weesh for no bettaire. But when I look at you, you do 'im *so*' – another even more vicious imitation. '*Eh, bien!* I no longer you regard. I turn ze back, *so*!' Deliberately he turned his back on me, and left me wishing that the floor would open and swallow me up.

To my astonishment, the class in general seemed to consider that I had received something in the nature of a decoration, instead of a reprimand. When the little man stopped to explain to the pianist how he wanted the music played, the girls gathered round me and whispered congratulations.

'Gosh, Jane – you *must* be good for him to fly out at you like that! He hardly ever does it to anyone éxcept Anna. He must be specially interested in you. Perhaps he'll throw his stick at you like Checcetti used to do! Shall you return it to him with a curtsy, if he does?'

'No, I'll fly for my life!' I whispered back. 'He scares me stiff!'

'Oh, he's a lamb, really!' they assured me. 'Just you wait till you hurt your foot or anything, he'll fuss over you like an old hen over a chicken! He's got the kindest heart in the world under all that temperamental stuff!'

After we had finished the *barre*-work, we did some exercises for centre-practice. Then we went on to *adage* and *enchainements*. I couldn't help feeling that, compared with the others, my *pirouettes* weren't bad, and several times my balance drew a word of praise from the Maestro. Mariella smiled at me encouragingly, which was decent of her because her own wobbles had been the occasion of more than one sarcastic comment from the little man.

'Mariella Foster! 'Ow much times 'ave I to tell you *not* to put down ze foot when you turn a *pirouette*? Vobble – he is bad; but to put down ze foot, he is verse. Much verse!'

At the end of the *enchainements* we were given a short breathing space. Then the little man announced: 'And now, we vill attempt once more ze Dance of ze Sugar Plum Fairy ... Ah! Ze leetle new one' (this was me) 'you do not know 'im, zis dance, no? You may rest zen – on ze floor.'

I stared at him in astonishment.

'Go on!' said Mariella, nudging me. 'He's having mercy on you; he's taken a fancy to you – I told you he had! You can have a breather, whilst we practise this horrible dance.'

'But he said *on the floor*!' I expostulated.

114

Mariella laughed.

'Well, that's all right. We're not allowed to sit down in class, you know – it makes your muscles contract. If you want to relax, you have to lie flat on the floor. Try it – it's ever so restful. Go on – be quick, before he changes his mind!'

After a moment's hesitation, I did as she said, and lay down on the floor at the back of the studio in as inconspicuous a place as possible, and nobody seemed the least surprised. From my lowly position I could no longer see the class, but above my head I heard the little Russian master haranguing it.

'Kat-leen! What do you there? *Mon Dieu!* But how you glitter! Your face, he is like ze advertisement for pan-shine one sees in ze Tube! Eef you are bright like zat at ze *commencement*, 'ow, zen, weel you ze climax achieve *à la fin*? Tell me zat! All life, he ees one beeg contrast – ze son, and zen ze shade. You are all son! I vipe my brow! *Regardez!*' In my imagination I saw the little man solemnly mop his forehead with a silk handkerchief he kept for this purpose.

'Chloë! Chloë!' his voice went on. 'You dance as eef ze Sugar Plum Fairy were a piece of Turkish delight half melted in ze mouth! Leesten, *leesten* to ze music! He is all clear-cut, like ze crystal – not sloosh! sloosh! like you make 'im . . . *Trés bien*, An-na! Zat ees good, zee *petits battements! Très bien!* But ze *gargouillardes* – *Gott in Himmel!* terribles, *mais terribles!* . . . Mariella! 'Ow much time have I point out to you ze shoulders. You strain zem! You leeft zem! Zey are not shoulders you 'ave there, but clothes-horses! *Mon Dieu*, Mariella, of you a dancer nevaire weel I make! . . .'

Over and over they practised the dance, whilst I lay at

my ease on the floor, relaxed. Groans, sighs, and panting breaths filled the studio.

'If we do those *gargouillardes* just once more, I'll die!' I heard Mariella say in a gasping voice from above me. 'Honestly, I just can't go through them again! Do you think he'd notice if I did *pas de chats* instead?'

'Try it and see!' laughed another voice with a rich Irish brogue.

'It's all very well for you, Kathleen,' came a third voice. 'You've got elevation!'

Fortunately, the Maestro suddenly tapped with his stick on the floor in a peremptory manner, announced solemnly to the class that his heart was broken, that after such an exhibition he found himself unable to continue – that, in other words, the lesson was over.

'He always says that,' Mariella said cheerfully, as we retired to the dressing-room. 'He must have a tough heart, the number of times it's been broken! Anyway, it's twenty minutes past the hour, the old humbug!'

Chapter 5

The Plot!

WE all talked at once as we stripped off tights and jock-belts, and pulled on our outdoor clothes.

'Gosh! What a beastly class!' Mariella exclaimed.

'Oh, I don't know—' This was Anna. 'I think it wasn't too bad, myself. Those *gargouillardes* got me down, though.'

'You mean they didn't get you up!' laughed Kathleen. 'Personally I think *gargouillardes* are rather fun. It's those *posés* into *arabesques* – you know, these things' – she demonstrated the position in question – 'that *I* can't do. I just don't seem to be able to stay on point. How do you do them, June – you seem to have got the knack?'

June was coaxing her hair back into its customary waves and curls.

'Oh, I don't know – it just comes,' she answered vaguely.

'Thanks for being so helpful!'

'It's funny,' I remarked, when there was a lull in the conversation, 'but I always imagined your Maestro to be as old as the dodo, Mariella. Why, he's quite young!'

'Thirty-five, to be exact,' came a chorus of voices. 'We worked it out by the ballets he was in.'

'Ballets?' I echoed. 'I didn't know he was a dancer.'

'Good gracious, yes!' said Mariella. 'Why, he was one of the greatest dancers in the world.'

'But why do you say "was"?' I questioned. 'If, as you

117

say, he's only thirty-five now, why isn't he still dancing? Surely thirty-five isn't so very old – for a man?'

'I see you don't know about Maestro,' said Chloë softly. 'I thought every dancer knew. He hurt his knee in *Les Patineurs* – split a tendon, or something. He's been to dozens of specialists, but they all say it's hopeless – he'll never dance again. It's an awful tragedy, because he just lives for it, and he had such wonderful elevation – they say the best since Nijinsky.'

'Have you ever seen him dance?' I asked her.

Chloë shook her head.

'Mummy has,' put in Mariella. 'In fact, he used to partner her. She was in the Wells Company when he was guest artist at Covent Garden the time he had the accident. They did *Les Patineurs*, as Chloë says, and after his solo as the Skater in Blue, he slipped on the stairs, and he never danced again. Mummy was the Girl in White in the classical *Pas de Deux*.'

My thoughts flew back to the time when I'd taken my Elementary RAD examination in Edinburgh last spring. The ballet had been at the Princes Theatre, and I'd seen this very ballet – *Les Patineurs*. I remembered the Exhibition Skater quite distinctly, and, although of course the dancer wasn't as wonderful as, by all accounts, Maestro had been, nevertheless he had made an impression on my mind. I pictured, now, the slender, skating figure, turning his endless *fouettes*, whilst the snowflakes fell softly all around him. Then I thought of Maestro, alone in the empty studio – Maestro, labouring day in, day out, to pass on his beloved Art to other people – Maestro, with his ascetic face, and his dynamic personality.

We went into Regent's Park on our way home as it was

too early for tea, and as we threw ourselves down on the grass near the lake, Mariella gave a sudden sigh.

'Gosh! There's that awful audition only just a week away!' she said, flinging a pebble gloomily into the water. 'I wish I could forget about the beastly thing, but I can't. It keeps butting in on my thoughts whenever I stop talking!'

'What I don't understand,' I said, in an effort to distract her attention, 'is why you have to go to Sadler's Wells at all. When you've got Madame whatever-her-name-is, and your wonderful Maestro to teach you, why can't you just stay here and go on learning with them? Or aren't they good enough?'

'It isn't a question of not being good enough,' explained Mariella, throwing a bit of biscuit to a passing duck. 'As a matter of fact, Mummy says that Madame and Maestro are two of the finest teachers in the world – bar none.'

'Well, then?' I persisted, watching the duck dabble the biscuit in the water to make it soft.

'But you see,' went on Mariella, 'one can't get direct on to the stage from Madame's school, however good she and Maestro may be. You must go to a school that's run in conjunction with a ballet. All first-class ballets have their own schools. Naturally, the Sadler's Wells Ballet is mostly "fed" from its own school.'

'Oh, I see—' I said slowly. 'I never thought of that. You mean, I couldn't go straight to Sadler's Wells from my Miss Martin's?'

Mariella shook her head.

'No – you'd have to go to the Wells School *after* your Miss Martin, if you see what I mean. But from what I've seen of your dancing, Jane, I think your Miss Martin is about the best person to get you to the Wells, if ever you really want to go.'

'I *do* want to go,' I said passionately. 'I want to go more than anything in the world. But tell me some more about Sadler's Wells, Mariella. Why has everyone who wants to get into their ballet got to go to their school?'

'Well, obviously they've got their own particular style,' answered Mariella a little impatiently. I think she was getting tired of my questions. 'And obviously there's only one place to acquire that style, and that's their own school. However wonderful Maestro is, his views don't always coincide with those of the Wells. In fact, he often disagrees most violently!'

'Yes, I can imagine that!' I laughed. 'Oh, Mariella, that was the most wonderful class I've ever had in my life, even if it *was* a bit frightening. Thank you, thank you for taking me!'

'That's OK,' said Mariella, throwing another bit of biscuit to the duck. 'You can go to several more classes if you like. There's still a week left – nearly.'

'What do you mean – still a week left?' I demanded.

'I mean a week to that stupid audition, of course,' said Mariella. 'Look, Jane – there's something I simply must tell you. I've been thinking – you aren't getting anywhere, you know, with your dancing, up there in Northumberland. Oh, it isn't that there's anything wrong with Northumberland, but it's your *people*. They're such dyed-in-the-wool huntin', shootin', and fishin' sort of people, if you know what I mean. They all expect you to become a veterinary surgeon, or a dog-breeder, and if you said you wanted to make dancing your career, they'd have a fit!'

'They certainly would!' I agreed.

120

'And even if your Miss Martin went to them and said that you were cut out to be a dancer, what would happen? They'd talk about the stage – spoken in a whisper, as if it were something indecent – being all very well for other people's daughters, but not for *their* daughter. They'd talk about "the temptations of Life behind the Footlights" and all that old-fashioned bosh. What you must do,' went on Mariella firmly before I had time to say anything, 'what you must do, Jane, is to present them with a *fait accompli*.'

'What's that?' I demanded.

'Oh, gosh! I forgot you didn't know any French – at least, not much,' Mariella said rather deprecatingly. 'A *fait accompli* means that you do something, and then, after it's safely done, you tell them about it.'

'Yes, but what have I got to *do*?' I asked, puzzled.

Mariella looked at the expectant duck, and then at the piece of biscuit in her hand; then she delivered the electric shock.

'Go to the audition on Friday,' she announced nonchalantly.

There was silence for a few minutes – shocked silence on my part; absorbed silence on the part of Mariella, since she had crammed the biscuit into her own mouth, and was crunching it with evident enjoyment. 'These shortbreads are jolly good,' she added. 'Better than I thought, or I shouldn't have been wasting them on the ducks!'

'Mariella,' I begged. 'Mariella – please – what did you say a minute ago? You didn't mean, did you, that I—'

'That you should go to the audition instead of me. That's right,' answered Mariella calmly. 'Why not?'

121

'But you can't go to an audition in someone else's place,' I declared. 'You just *can't*!'

'Why not?' said Mariella again. 'They're out for wonderful dancers for their ballet, aren't they? Well, *you* are going to be a wonderful dancer. They'll know it when they see you. *I* knew it when we practised together yesterday, and now that class today – Maestro – he knew it, too.'

'But, Mariella,' I expostulated, 'they'd know I wasn't you.'

'Not they,' contradicted Mariella. 'I've never been there – never seen one of them. They know Mummy, naturally, but that's all to the good. In fact I was wondering what on earth would happen when *I* walked in – red hair and all. Oh, yes – it *is* red although kind people call it auburn! Now when you turn up, looking the very image of Mummy, because you know you *are*, Jane, they'll just fall upon your neck!'

'But I might have to sign forms and things,' I objected.

'Really, Jane – you *are* dense!' declared Mariella. 'If you have to sign anything, you sign it, of course – J. M. Foster. Your name is Jane Monkhouse Foster; mine is Juanita Mariella Foster. Our initials are the same. My surname is really Devereux, of course, like Daddy's, but I always use Mummy's stage name – Foster – even when I sign things. So you see it's perfectly all right – I've thought it all out. There isn't a snag anywhere.'

'Yes, there is,' I persisted. 'It's wrong to impersonate someone else.'

'It's not doing anyone any harm,' declared Mariella. 'After it's over, and you're in, we'll tell them about it, and I can have a shot at getting in myself. But the important point is that you'll be able to say to your people: "By the way – while I was in London I had an audition for the Sadler's Wells School, and I got in. You don't mind, do you?" What can they say?'

'Lots!' I said prophetically.

'What? When you tell them you've been accepted by the most famous ballet school in the world?' said Mariella. 'They won't stand out for long! You know, Jane,' she added earnestly, 'you'll have to get an awful lot more *tough* if you're going to get anywhere in ballet. You'll have to set your heart on it and stop at nothing – *nothing*, Jane. If you're going to be a dancer – and I know you *are* going to be one – that's what you must do. It's funny that, although I hate it as a career for myself, yet I can still enthuse about other people's ability! I know when they're good and when they're not. I suppose it's Daddy coming out in me! Why, even the way you're sitting now, Jane – you look like one of the Cygnets in *Swan Lake*. Everything you do, and every way you sit is graceful.'

I sat there for a long time, while the duck, evidently tired of waiting for biscuits, dived into the water. I stared absent-mindedly at its back end and yellow feet sticking up in the air; then I drew a deep breath.

'I'll do it!' I promised. 'It's funny, Mariella, to be plotting this tremendous thing out here in the sunlight, with lots of people everywhere, and ducks quacking, and everything terribly un-mysterious, if you see what I mean. We ought, by rights, to be doing it in a cellar at dead of night by the light of a single, guttering candle!'

'How like you to think of something romantic like that!' laughed Mariella. 'You're always *thinking*, Jane, whereas I like *doing* things – riding to hounds, for instance.'

123

'Well, *you've* never ridden to hounds, have you?' I retorted.

'Only in books so far,' admitted Mariella sadly. 'But you bet I'll be doing it in actual fact before very long. You can do anything if you set your mind to it.'

'What a pity we haven't a bottle of lemonade handy!' I laughed. 'We could have drunk to our dreams ... Oh, but we *can*!' I ran down to the edge of the water and scooped some up in my hands.

'Oh, not *that* water, Jane!' cried Mariella in disgust. 'Why, the ducks have been paddling in it!'

Regretfully I let the water trickle down upon the ground.

'Yes, you're right – I suppose they have. Never mind – we'll *pretend* we've drunk it ... Here's to the hounds for you, Mariella! And here's to the audition for me! May both our dreams come true!'

Chapter 6

The Plot Thickens!

THE week flew by as if on wings. Before I realized it, Friday had arrived – Friday, the day of my audition!

Mariella took me by Underground to 45 Colet Gardens, where the Sadler's Wells School is, and left me outside the door.

'Go on, Jane! And good luck!' she whispered, giving me a little push. 'And don't forget – if they ask you what your name is, just say "J. M. Foster". Goodbye! I'll be here at four o'clock to pick up the pieces!'

The next hour or so was more like a dream than anything else. Time seemed to stand still; the world, outside the portals of 45 Colet Gardens, ceased to exist for me. When I emerged at four o'clock, I felt as if I had been on a trip to the moon, or some other unknown planet, or as if I had been asleep for a hundred years like the princess in the fairy tale and had just wakened up.

Mariella had kept her promise, and was waiting for me outside. We walked down the road a little way, and then turned aside on to a piece of wasteland near Cadby Hall.

'Well, let's hear about it,' said Mariella, seating herself on the edge of a wall. 'I've brought some chocolate and a packet of biscuits. I thought you might need them!'

'I do! I'm so hungry I could eat a horse!' I exclaimed, sitting down beside her.

'To begin with,' went on Mariella, 'have you – I mean

I – golly! Really, I don't know what I *do* mean!'

'You mean, have I got in? Or have you?' I laughed. 'Yes, one of us has, and I expect it's me really, only it's you who'll be taking the place, worse luck! They told me it was OK before I came away, and it'll be confirmed in a day or two. I'm to start on Monday – I mean *you* are.'

'Well – how did you like it?' demanded Mariella. 'Was it too awful for words?'

'Awful?' I echoed, aghast. 'It was *wonderful*! You just don't know how wonderful it was! And to think, Mariella, that it actually happened to *me*!'

Mariella shrugged her shoulders expressively, a habit she had caught from Aunt Irma, I think.

'Begin at the beginning, Jane,' she ordered. 'And don't keep on saying "*wonderful*" like that all the time! After you left me, what did you do?'

'I walked in at the pupils' entrance,' I answered. 'Inside, it was something like a conservatory, only no plants and things – only little green chairs and tables. They call it the Winter Garden, by the way. I found the girls' dressing-room all right – it's down some stone stairs facing you as you go in the Winter Garden door. There were an awful lot of girls in the dressing-room, and of course they stared like anything. Some of them took no notice of me, but some were ever so helpful. My audition was just in an ordinary class – I mean, I was told to join in at the back. Someone called Gilbert Delahaye took the class, and there were several other people there as well – two ladies, one fair, and one dark, and a small, dark man.'

'And I suppose they fell all over you?' said Mariella. 'In other words, proclaimed you as a star, straight away.'

I missed the sarcasm in her voice.

126

'Oh, *no*!' I said, shocked at the very idea. 'They didn't take the least bit of notice of me, as a matter of fact.'

Mariella burst out laughing.

'I thought you said it was a wonderful class?' she teased.

'So it was,' I said earnestly. 'Just to be there at all was wonderful. I kept saying to myself: "This is the Baylis Hall, where Margot Fonteyn worked!" Then I remembered that Colet Gardens hasn't housed the Sadler's Wells School for very long – only a year or two – so Margot Fonteyn couldn't have worked there. It was a great disappointment! However, I said to myself: "Well, never mind, this is probably the very same *barre* where Veronica Weston did her *barre*-work." I know *she* worked here because I read all about it in her biography.'

'Oh – you mean the one Daddy wrote?' put in Mariella, carefully breaking the bar of chocolate into two equal pieces, and dividing up the biscuits – there were four each. 'Gosh! What fun we had over that! I must say Daddy can be amusing when he likes! Do you remember the chapter where he says he first saw Veronica? It was at the Zoo on a Sunday morning, and she was haring after a red-headed boy who'd been ill-treating her pet monkey. Daddy said she was coming down the straight like a Derby winner, and she nearly knocked him flat! And you know the famous choreographer, Toni Rossini? He wasn't famous then, and he was following on behind, imploring Veronica to stop. "Please, Veronique—" he was saying in his beautiful, polite, foreign voice. "Please, Veronique – I beg of you to stop!"'

'And did she?' I asked.

'Not Veronica! She just rode on over Daddy's prostrate body – that's how he describes it! – caught up the boy, and pushed him flat in the pelicans' pond, all among the pelicans!'

'Gosh! How glorious! Good for Veronica! I must say I think the awful boy deserved it!' I exclaimed.

'Yes, he did, didn't he!' laughed Mariella. 'But go on, Jane. You were telling me about the audition. Didn't anyone say *anything* to you?'

'Oh, yes – they asked a lot of questions,' I answered. 'Fortunately they were mostly about *me* – my feet, and so on – so I was able to answer quite truthfully. They didn't go into family details, thank goodness!'

'It seems to me,' said Mariella when we had finished the biscuits, 'that we ought to have a real celebration. You can't call half a bar of chocolate and four shortbreads a real celebration. Let's go to Lyons Corner House at Marble Arch and have tea; they've got lots of lovely, squashy cakes and jolly nice ice-cream. And after we've had tea, let's go into Hyde Park and watch the people riding.'

'All right,' I agreed. Although I didn't consider watching people riding much of a treat, I hadn't the heart to tell Mariella so. And, after all, the audition had been her idea in the first place, so I felt that she ought to have most say in how we celebrated my victory – if you could call it that!

As a matter of fact, there weren't any riders in the Park, or if there were they didn't come in our direction. So Mariella and I just sat in the sun and talked.

'Now I've got over the terrific thrill of the audition, I'm beginning to feel most awfully sad,' I confessed, drawing a picture of a ballet dancer on the back of the dusty seat with the tip of my finger. 'Sad, I mean, because although I've got the right to attend that gorgeous

128

school, I still can't go to it because of my people. Oh, Mariella – isn't it awful!'

'It needn't be,' said Mariella calmly. 'I don't see why you shouldn't go – for a bit, anyway.'

'But of course we must confess everything,' I said firmly, 'We arranged that when we first thought of the idea.'

'Of course we'll have to confess,' agreed Mariella, drawing a prancing horse alongside my ballet dancer. 'But not just yet. After all, there are still three whole weeks – no, a month – before you go home, and there's nothing exciting to do in London – absolutely nothing. Besides, if you don't go to those beastly classes, *I* can't go to them either, because I haven't passed my audition. So poor Daddy's money will be wasted, and I'm sure you wouldn't like that, Jane. Yes, and think of the agony you'll save me from. Those beastly classes—'

'But you said just now that you couldn't go to them?' I protested. 'Leaving me out of it.'

'Well, no, I couldn't,' admitted Mariella. 'But think, Jane – think of the glorious three weeks' holiday I shall have if you go instead. I shan't have to go back to Maestro, because *he'll* think I'm at the Wells. I shall be able to read all my pony books over again. Oh, Jane – please be unselfish and do it!'

I was beginning to get to know Mariella by now. She was like Nigel – so used to getting her own way, that she almost always got it! She did so now.

'All right,' I said. 'I know it's all wrong. I know it's frightful of me, but I'll do it.'

Chapter 7

Mariella Meets a Friend

'WE'VE got the whole weekend free – before you start at the Wells, I mean,' Mariella said next morning. We were having breakfast together in the lounge – just the two of us. Uncle Oscar was working in his study and didn't want to be disturbed, so he'd had his breakfast sent in to him. 'What shall we do?'

I thought deeply.

'Yes, it is a problem, isn't it?' said Mariella naughtily. 'What does one do in London at the weekend? Go to the pictures; walk in the Park; go shopping! ... Now you see how ghastly it is for me, Jane!'

'I wasn't thinking that at all,' I told her. 'As a matter of fact, I was thinking what a lot of things you *could* do, and the trouble was to decide which.'

'Trot them out, then,' said Mariella, 'and I'll choose the least boring.'

'Well, we could go to the Tate Gallery, and look at the pictures,' I began. 'There are some by Degas – ballet ones : Daddy told me about them – and Dame Laura Knight—'

'Filthy!' burst out Mariella. 'Go on!'

'We could go and just *look* at the outside of Covent Garden,' I said dreamily.

'Too thrilling for words – I *don't* think!' pronounced Mariella. 'Not for me, thank you, Jane! It's the dirtiest place you ever saw in your life is Covent Garden on the *outside.* And you can smell it a mile off – the cabbages and things!'

'Yes, but think of all the wonderful people who have walked in and out of its stage door!' I exclaimed. 'I think the very name, Covent Garden, is the most romantic name on earth!'

'Like Newmarket is to me,' said Mariella slowly. 'Or Aintree. In a way, I can see what you mean, Jane. But really, I refuse to spend the entire weekend just looking at the outside of Covent Garden – not even to please you! Any more suggestions?'

'Well, couldn't we go *inside*, then,' I suggested wistfully. 'To the evening performance, I mean. We could go in the gallery slips; Daddy says they're not too ruinously expensive. He says he often used to go there in his young days.'

'Oh, all right,' agreed Mariella. 'Anything for a quiet life! But anyway, that's for tonight. What shall we do this morning?'

'I know!' I exclaimed. 'Let's go to Harrods – that shop where you buy your lovely clothes. I've always wanted to see it.'

Mariella gave a hoot of laughter.

'What? Spend Saturday morning in Harrods. *Quelle drôle idée!* as Mummy would say! No – *I'll* tell you what we'll do; we'll go swimming.'

I might have known that, in the end, Mariella would decide what we were going to do. She collected up a couple of towels, and two wonderful swimsuits which had 'Harrods' written all over them. One was sea-green 'so as not to make my hair look too awful,' she said, and the other was plain black.

Fortunately, there was a swimming bath not very far

131

away from Fortnum Mansions, and it only took us a few minutes to get there. At just ten o'clock, we were walking up the steps, our swimming things tucked under our arms.

'It's so early there won't be a crush,' said Mariella as we bought our tickets.

When I came out of my cubicle, in answer to Mariella's 'Are you ready, Jane?' the first thing I saw was a young man standing on the highest diving-board at the end farthest away from me. As I watched him, he dived.

'Oh, Mariella!' I exclaimed in a whisper. 'What a wonderful dive! I've never seen anyone look like that when they dived. He looked like one of those photographs in the book Cousin Marjorie sent me for my birthday last year.'

'Glad you think he looks OK,' laughed Mariella, 'because he's a friend of mine ... Hullo, Josef!' she shouted so as to be heard above the noise of the swimming bath. 'Taking some exercise?'

The young man, who had been swimming as effortlessly and as gracefully as a fish, drew himself out of the water at her words, and stood before us. He was indeed a splendid young man – like a slender, bronze statue. I couldn't help looking at him with admiration, as though he were a picture. His black hair was crinkled with the water, and drops of water glistened upon his finely muscled arms and shoulders. He reminded me, in his grace and strength, of a tiger or a leopard. He looked as if he had never performed an ungraceful action in all his life.

'Josef – this is my cousin Jane,' said Mariella. 'Jane is already a "fan". She thinks you dive frightfully well!'

The young man bowed from the waist, and how he

managed to look dignified clad only in a pair of bathing-trunks, and wet at that, I don't know, but he did!

'*Enchanté*,' he murmured, and then something else that I didn't understand.

'You're wasting your sweetness – I mean your compliments – on the desert air, Josef!' pronounced Mariella. 'Jane doesn't understand French. By the way,' she added, without giving the young man time to say anything, 'Josef used to go to my dancing school, didn't you, Josef? It was a long, long time ago – before my time, in fact.'

The young man's slightly slanting, dark eyes dwelt slumberously upon Mariella's bright curls.

'One of these days I shall take great pleasure in giving you a good beating!' he threatened. '*Méchante* child!'

'Not in England you won't!' laughed Mariella with a toss of her curls. 'In the savage country where you come from you might, but here, in England, girls don't get beaten.'

'Ah! Then perhaps *this* will suffice,' said Josef. He lunged towards Mariella, and sent her flat on her back into the pool.

Mariella didn't seem to be at all annoyed at being treated so unceremoniously. In fact, I felt all the time that she understood the young man, and he, her. She laughed up at us, and swam away.

'And now that we have rid ourselves of the *enfant terrible*, how shall we amuse ourselves?' asked my new acquaintance. 'Do you play water polo?' He nodded towards a group of people who were playing about at the deep end with a gaily striped ball.

'Oh, no! I'm not nearly good enough for that!' I exclaimed. 'Couldn't you – wouldn't you dive again for me? I love to see you dive.'

'With pleasure,' said the young man. '*Enchanté!* Excuse, please!' This to a group of girls who were standing on the edge trying to make up their minds to jump in. He made his way to the diving-board, climbed to the highest platform, poised there for a moment, and then dived in — a beautiful swallow dive this time. He was really most obliging, and did it several times for my especial benefit. When at last he came back to my side, I thanked him profusely.

'It's really most awfully nice of you to go to all that trouble especially for me,' I said.

'Oh, don't worry!' came Mariella's voice from behind us. 'Josef likes showing off. In fact he lives for it!'

'If you will float on the water,' said Josef, ignoring Mariella's remark, 'I will dive underneath. I promise I will not so much as ripple the water into your mouth!'

'Having a good time, aren't you, Josef?' shouted Mariella from the shallow end where she was trying to walk along the bottom of the swimming bath on her hands. 'Someone to show all your little tricks to! Don't encourage him, Jane. You'll make him even more conceited than he is already, if that were possible!'

'Do not of her take any notice,' said the young man, turning his back upon the irrepressible Mariella. 'See, I mount the platform! Arrange yourself upon the water — so!' He made an expressive gesture which told me to lie down flat. '*Attention!* I dive!'

He did so, making scarcely a ripple upon the surface of the water. I sat up, and saw to my surprise that all the polo players had stopped their game, and were watching; as also the timid girls standing upon the edge. It was plain that this young man could command attention merely by the force of his personality. After all, a high dive in a swimming bath, however good it might be, wasn't really so very spectacular. If any ordinary person had done it, it wouldn't have made anyone even look round.

We said goodbye to Mariella's friend on the steps outside the main entrance.

'Well, *au revoir*, Josef!' said Mariella. 'By the way, Jane is a dancer too, you know. She's going to be very famous. Oh, you can smile, but I *know*! Mark my words, as Daddy would say – there'll come a day when you'll be proud to boast that you dived underneath the famous Jane Foster at the swimming bath! Yes – even you, Josef Linsk!'

'Mariella!' I exclaimed, as the young man went on his way. 'You don't mean to say that that young man was really Josef Linsk?'

'Yes, really!' said Mariella mockingly. 'Why shouldn't he be?'

'But Josef Linsk!' I wailed. 'The world-famous dancer! I ought to have taken more notice of him. I ought to have been more *respectful*. You might have *told* me, Mariella!'

'Well, I thought you'd know,' answered Mariella casually. 'I did say his name was Josef, didn't I? Only one Josef in the world – according to Linsk, anyway!'

'I can't help wondering why you were so rude to him,' I said curiously. 'You *were* rude, you know, Mariella. Dreadfully!'

'Was I?' Unconcernedly Mariella unrolled her towel, and then rolled it up again more tidily. 'As a matter of fact, there's a – I can't think of the word, but it means a sort of hatred between us.'

'But why?' I persisted.

135

Mariella tucked her arm through mine, and set off down the road.

'I'll tell you,' she said. 'Josef Linsk was the dancer who took Maestro's place in *Spectre de la Rose* that awful night – I mean the night of Maestro's accident. We were all at the theatre. Mummy was dancing in *Patineurs*, and Daddy and I were sitting in the stalls. When it happened, Daddy got to know straight away, naturally. We both went round behind to find out how serious it was, and *he* was there' – she nodded in the direction Josef Linsk had taken.

'Well, what about it?' I asked. 'He couldn't help having to take Maestro's place, could he?'

'No,' said Mariella. 'But he *could* help the beastly, self-satisfied, *pleased* look on his face when he saw poor Maestro carried out on the stretcher. I shall never, never forgive him! As if Joseph Linsk was any substitute for Ivan Stcherbakof – that's Maestro's name, you know. Oh I believe I told you. Anyway, he's horribly conceited. I hate conceited people!'

'Nigel's conceited,' I said slowly. 'You don't hate Nigel.'

'Nigel's not conceited a bit!' flared up Mariella. 'He can do things, and he knows it. That's not being conceited.'

As we neared Fortnum Mansions I couldn't help feeling that there was a lot in something Daddy once said – that if you like a person, it doesn't matter what they do, or what faults they have, you make them all into virtues, and vice versa.

Chapter 8

Masquerade!

I STARTED at the Wells on the following Monday, and, as Mariella had predicted everything went well. Nobody asked awkward questions, and I got quite used to being called 'Mariella'! As for Uncle Oscar, I don't believe he even missed me. He was very busy at the moment cataloguing some jade ornaments he had picked up at a sale, and he spent nearly all his time in his study with his head in a glass showcase. At least, Mariella told me so when I asked her whether her father didn't think it strange that I had disappeared.

'Oh, Daddy's forgotten you're staying here, I expect!' she laughed. 'Or perhaps he thinks you've gone home. He's like that – especially when he's got what I call a "jade spell" on! And by the way, that letter of confirmation about your audition came – I know it was it because it was typewritten and it had a South Kensington postmark on it. It was addressed to Mummy, so it's been sent on to her to New Zealand with the rest of her mail. So that's all right! I was a bit worried about that letter,' admitted Mariella.

'And what about you?' I asked. We were having tea, and I'd been at the Wells for about a week. 'Isn't it frightfully boring for you, being here all by yourself?'

'Boring? Golly, no! I'm having a super time,' Mariella assured me. 'No Miss Linton, no Osbert Darlington to chivvy me about my Latin. Nothing to do all day but read your Wendy books, and go to the swimming baths, and watch the people riding in the Park. What bliss! Wouldn't it be wonderful if it could go on for ever!'

'Well, it can't,' I said. 'Mariella – it's going to be awful at the end of my holiday when we have to confess.'

'Don't worry!' Mariella said easily. 'I'll do it. You can trip out of the Sadler's Wells School on the Saturday morning, after your class, and dash off back to Northumberland. Then I'll trip back to the Wells on the Monday to receive the fireworks!'

'U-um,' I said doubtfully. 'You don't know Mr Delahaye, our ballet master, or Miss Willan, the head mistress of the ballet part of the school, or the DIRECTOR!'

'Gosh! You make him sound like a bluebeard!' laughed Mariella.

'But he *is* – oh, I don't mean he's got a room with umpteen dead wives in it, but he's – well, he's the *Director*!'

'Well, what if he is?' scoffed Mariella. 'He can't *eat* you! He can't even expel you, because you'll already be expelled – self-expelled – and he can't expel *me*, because I'm not accepted yet. Marvellous, isn't it?'

'Yes, it is,' I said unhappily. I couldn't help feeling that Mariella hadn't felt the atmosphere of the Wells. The thing I had done seemed to get worse every minute. To gatecrash into the Sadler's Wells School – unheard of! I felt sure that no one had ever done it before – and no one ever would again. Not after me!

'Oh, well – stop getting into a flap about it!' begged Mariella. ' "Sufficient unto the day is the evil thereof," as Shakespeare says, or is it the Bible? Let's hear what you do at your gloomy school, and who you meet. I shall probably be going there myself before long – worse luck!

138

– so I may as well know the worst! How many students are there in your class, and what time do you begin work?'

'I'm in the Junior class of the Senior School,' I explained. 'We don't begin so early just now because the educational classes don't start till the end of September, when the other part of the school does. There are about twenty students in my ordinary ballet class, and the person who teaches us most is Gilbert – Gilbert Delahaye, I mean. He's English, but he's frightfully temperamental, so that sometimes you'd think he wasn't. We all *adore* Gilbert, and the Senior class is frightfully jealous because we have him most of the time. Everyone wants Gilbert! Of course, he's got a temper and throws things, but that's what you expect in a great teacher of ballet, isn't it?'

'Don't I know it?' sighed Mariella. 'Haven't I had umpteen years with Maestro! Well, tell me what the people you're with are like.'

As we ate our tea, I told Mariella about the students – Canadian Sadie and Isobel, and Lotus Flower (that was what her name meant in English; we called her Lotus for short), the Cingalese girl who was going back to Ceylon to teach dancing. I told her about Carmencita Rosita Fernandez, who was twenty-two and married.

'She's already a famous dancer in her own country,' I explained. 'But she's come over here to the Wells to learn something about classical ballet. She's a perfect darling. Everyone loves Carmen – especially Serge Lopokoff – he's the Russian master who takes the Character classes.'

'What's she like to look at?' demanded Mariella, sadly declining my offer of a chocolate éclair. 'Sorry! Bad for my hips! *You* have it, Jane.'

139

'Oh, she's wonderful,' I answered, taking a large bite out of the éclair, so that the cream squashed out in all directions. 'She's got blue-black hair, and a very white centre parting, and huge, slumberous dark eyes that flash fire one minute, and melt the next! She comes up to you and puts her arms round you and says: "Dar-leeng! 'Ow I lov' you!" I believe she does, too!'

'Aren't there any English girls?' asked Mariella.

'Oh, yes – quite a few, though I must say an awful lot of the students seem to be from the Colonies,' I answered. 'But there are several Irish girls, and one Welsh in my class, and my best friend – Janet Sanderson – is Scottish. Her name sounds plain, but she's frightfully pretty herself – tiny, and dark, and very vivacious... Mariella! I don't believe you've been listening to a word I've said!'

'Oh, yes I have,' said Mariella. 'On and off! But let's do something *interesting* now, shall we? Let's go to the pictures.'

'I thought you didn't like pictures,' I objected. 'Besides, I've got some point shoes to darn.'

'Oh, you can do them tomorrow,' declared Mariella, characteristically brushing the objection aside. 'As a matter of fact, you're right – I'm not too keen about the pictures – not ordinary ones, I mean. But there's a film all about racehorses at Studio One – I saw the pictures of it. It ought to be marvellous! Come on, Jane!'

I had been at the Wells three weeks when the blow fell. I hadn't the slightest warning that it was going to fall, and when the swing door of the Baylis Hall opened that afternoon, just at the end of Gilbert Delahaye's class, and two ladies walked in, I hardly even turned my head. One of

140

the newcomers was Miss Willan, the principal, and the other was a visitor.

'Lady Bailey!' I heard whispered round the class. 'She's always coming in to watch. Look out for squalls! She always gets Gilbert's rag out!'

'The same exercise again, please,' ordered Gilbert, nodding to the pianist. 'A little more as if you were *dancers* – not football players! Ready! Begin! ... One-and-two...'

I saw that someone had got a chair for Lady Bailey, and that Miss Willan had gone. I also saw that Gilbert's brows were drawn together in a fine scowl – he hated anyone to watch his classes, and, as Janet had whispered to me, Lady Bailey was his *bête noire*. I knew instinctively that Lady Bailey irritated him – from her good-natured, fat face, to her expensive, high-heeled shoes.

For the remainder of the class he gave us all the dullest exercises and least showy *enchainements* he could think of. We did all the things we hated most, like *pirouettes* by quarter-turns, *petits battements sautés*, and the preparation for flik-flak, instead of exciting *fouettés* and *cabrioles*. Gilbert was certainly no angel upon occasions!

Just at the end of the class, Lady Bailey, sweetly smiling, and murmuring inane things about 'the dear children' – meaning us! – dropped the bombshell!

'Oh, by the way, I've just remembered,' she twittered, 'my friend Irma Foster's little girl is in this school, isn't she? Now, let me see – where is she? I suppose she *is* in this class?' She raised her lorgnette and peered at us through it. 'Not in the front row—'

'Mariella! Come here!' snapped Gilbert.

For a moment I hesitated.

141

'Mariella! I said come here!' repeated Gilbert. 'Are you deaf, or can't I speak plain English?'

I hesitated no longer. Dashing through two rows of astonished girls, I reached the nearest door, and fled. I dashed down the staircase – fortunately the stairs had rubber stuff on them to stop you slipping – and I didn't stop running until I reached the safety of our dressing-room. Once there I sank on to a form and panted, wondering what on earth I should do. In a moment or two the rest of the class appeared.

'Golly, Mariella! What on earth did you do that for?' Sylvia exclaimed. 'Gilbert is roaring like a bull! That woman always upsets him; she's tellling him about the time when she was in the chorus at the Windmill or somewhere, where she met Sir Eustace Bailey, and now *you*!— He says you're to go back at once. *At once!*' Wickedly Sylvia mimicked Gilbert in his wrath. 'Gosh! I wouldn't be you!'

'Neither would I!' I thought. 'Not if I could be anybody else at this present moment!' I went slowly back up the stairs to the Baylis Hall; it was like walking to the scaffold! Suddenly I felt that I had done a very stupid thing in running away like that. After all, Lady Bailey probably didn't know Mariella well. She mightn't even know her at all, personally. I might have been able to pass off as my cousin all right. With all my heart I wished I could re-live that last ten minutes, but of course it wasn't the least use wishing. I just had to go in and face the music.

'Well, Mariella,' said Gilbert in his most sarcastic voice, 'may I ask to what we owe this excessive show of good manners?'

'I'm very sorry, Mr Delahaye,' I said, keeping as far

142

away from Lady Bailey as I could. 'I – I didn't feel very well.'

'Strange,' commented Gilbert, obviously unbelieving. 'I had just been watching you, and thinking how very well you looked. Are you quite recovered now.'

'Yes – I think so – thank you,' I murmured.

'Good!' exclaimed Gilbert. 'Then you will please give us a little exhibition of ballet technique – especially for the benefit of Lady Bailey here. She tells me she dotes on ballet. Let us show her some. An *enchainement*, please. Just go on until I tell you to stop.'

He gave the *enchainement* – a terrible dull and ugly one; I marked it out dutifully; the pianist gave me a sympathetic glance – she was a firm friend of mine. Then I began.

Over and over I did that *enchainement*, and Lady Bailey watched. Gilbert sat at the edge of the stage, tapping the toe of his tennis shoe with his stick. It was awful! The *enchainement* was one of those you could do nothing with; there wasn't a single lovely movement in it – or so it seemed to me.

'Not always so very graceful, is it?' Gilbert said, looking down at his visitor. 'Go on, Mariella; we are enthralled by this charming exhibition!'

Through the music I heard Lady Bailey murmur something about: 'It's not often that the talent of the parent descends upon the child, is it, Mr Delahaye?'

My blood rose. I'd show her whether I had talent or not! I'd jolly well show her!

'*Stop!*' I shouted to the astonished pianist. 'Lady Bailey – I *can* dance when I'm given something decent to do. I can! I can! ... Look! This is the Dance of the Sugar Plum Fairy.' I began the opening *posés*. Under my eyelashes I saw Gilbert open his mouth to order me to stop. Then he didn't; he just sat still on the edge of the stage, looking at me. The friendly pianist picked up the music and accompanied me beautifully.

I forgot all about Lady Bailey, and Gilbert's hateful sarcasm; I completely forgot where I was, and the awful blow that was surely going to fall upon me before another hour was over; I forgot everything. I just danced ... As I executed the well-known steps, I imagined a vast, pillared hall, lit by a thousand winking candles. The floor was ice, and the roof was the wintry sky, studded with frost-bright stars. From each star hung a trembling icicle, and every now and then a tiny piece of ice would fall from one of them on to the shining floor with a musical tinkle. In the middle of the hall stood a beautiful Christmas tree, with frosted branches outspread. The boughs were hung with all kinds of sweetmeats – pink and white Turkish delight; stripy mint sweets : delicate fondant creams; toffee-apples; pale sugared almonds; pink coconut-ice; green crême-de-menthe... And I was the Sugar Plum Fairy, who had created this feast by one wave of her magic wand.

Beyond the lighted hall stretched a mighty forest, deep in snow and ice. It was dark out there, with only the Aurora Borealis, flooding across the northern sky, to light the tops of the fir trees. Deep in the lonely forest neither the starlight nor the flickering Northern Lights could penetrate...

I had just got as far as this, and was about to dance out into the trackless forest when the dance ended, and I was brought down to earth – or rather, to the Baylis Hall – with a bump

'Very nice!' Gilbert said, and this time there was no

sarcasm at all in his voice. 'Well, as you see, Lady Bailey, Mariella has perhaps inherited some small part of her mother's talent.'

But Lady Bailey wasn't listening to him. To my horror she was staring at me with a pucker between her plucked eyebrows, her lorgnette up to her short-sighted eyes.

'But this – *this* is not Mariella.'

'Mariella Foster is the name,' Gilbert said wearily – he'd had more than enough of Lady Bailey. 'I thought you said you knew her?'

'So I do,' said Lady Bailey. 'But this is not Mariella Foster.'

'Oh, yes,' said Gilbert patiently. 'Yes, it is.'

'Don't argue with me, young man!' snapped Lady Bailey. 'I've known Mariella ever since she was born. I had tea with her only a few weeks ago. I saw her in Madame Jacques' hat shop just the other day. You're not Mariella, are you, dear?'

Something gave way inside me. I knew I was found out – well, I'd expected that sooner or later. But to be unmasked by this horrible old woman with the too-tight shoes, and the too-large fur coat. It was awful!

'No, I'm not Mariella!' I yelled at her. 'I'm Jane! Jane! *Jane!*' My voice rose with each word.

Then I tore off my ballet shoes, and flung them down at her feet.

'Now look what you've done to me!' I sobbed. 'Look what you've done! You've ruined my life! You've spoilt everything! I shall never dance again!'

'Mariella! Stop this minute!' ordered Gilbert sternly, sounding frightfully astonished. 'How dare you!'

I turned upon him.

'I'm *not* Mariella!' I yelled at him. 'Didn't you hear

145

what she said? I'm *Jane*! She's quite right, and I'm going home!'

I turned my back on them and fled, tears streaming from my eyes. As I went, I heard Gilbert murmur an apology to Lady Bailey, and say something about 'these temperamental girls'.

As I dashed toward the swing doors I saw, out of the corner of my eye, that someone was sitting on the balcony, and that the someone was no less a person than the Director of the school himself!

'What on earth's happened?' said a chorus of voices as I flung myself on to a form in the dressing-room. 'Gosh! Was he as furious as all that?'

'I – I don't know!' I sobbed.

'Don't know? ...' Gloria Higgins stared at me in astonishment. Gloria was a pretty, rather hard-faced girl. She wasn't one of my special friends, and I had always thought her somewhat supercilious. 'How do you mean – *don't know*?'

I dried my eyes on somebody's tights that were lying beside me on the bench, and gave a loud sniff of self-pity.

'He seemed more astonished than furious when I yelled at him that I wasn't Mariella—'

'What?' came a chorus of voices. 'You yelled *what*?'

'That I wasn't Mariella,' I repeated firmly. 'And I'm not; I'm Jane. I'm Jane Foster – Mariella's cousin, and I came to the audition in her place.'

As you can imagine, there was a positive furore after this announcement.

'Come on – tell us about it,' Gloria commanded.

So I told them all about everything – about how

146

Mariella had come to Monks Hollow, my home in the country; about my first dancing lessons with Miss Martin. Finally I told them about Mariella's idea that we should change places.

'You see,' I explained, 'Mariella doesn't really like dancing. She'd much rather be a vet, and mess about with animals.'

'Sounds as if she's got a lot of sense,' said Gloria, with a grimace. 'A dancer's life is a dog's life, anyway. If she likes doing it, it's just bearable; if she doesn't, it's—'

Her words were cut off abruptly by the door opening, and a voice – the voice of the Director's secretary – saying cheerfully:

'Mariella Foster! The Director wants to see you in his office and you'd better hurry up – it's nearly lunchtime!'

'Oh, well,' I said as I got up, 'I knew this had to come; it's just a bit sooner than I expected, that's all. I wouldn't care if only it hadn't been that revolting old hag who'd given the game away – Lady Bailey, I mean.'

'Look here – hadn't you better put a spot of powder on your nose?' Gloria said. 'It's shining like the morning sun! Here – have some of mine.'

I shook my head miserably.

'No thank you – I don't feel it matters.' All the same I was grateful for her kindness. It was so unexpected, coming from a girl like Gloria.

'Keep your pecker up, honey,' said Sadie. 'He can't *eat* you!'

'That's what Mariella said!' I answered with a watery smile. But somehow it wasn't much of a consolation to know that it was true. It wasn't the row I minded, but the fact that I'd be sent away in disgrace – that I would never be allowed to have another class with dear Gilbert, or Serge, or indeed any of them. It was a dreadful thought.

I came out of the Director's office weeping like a fountain. At the door of the dressing-room an awestruck crowd of girls met me.

'Mariella — I mean, Jane! What did he say? ... Was he livid? ... Did he tear you limb from limb? ... Shall you be turned out on the spot? ...' Questions rained down on me like machine-gun bullets. 'Dar-leeng! My 'eart he bleed for you!' This, needless to say, was Carmencita, the Spanish girl. 'The Director I will beard in his lair for you! I go! I intercede for you, yes?'

'It — it's all r-right!' I hiccoughed, stopping Carmen just in time from departing on her errand of mercy. 'Everything's all r-right! He w-wasn't livid at all. He w-was a perfect l-lamb!'

'And you're *not* going to be turned out?'

'No-no.'

'Then,' said Canadian Sadie, pulling hairgrips out of her hair at lightning speed, 'what on earth are you crying for?'

'I'm crying because I can't h-help it,' I sobbed. 'I'm crying because I'm so h-happy!'

'Seems a crazy idea to me,' pronounced the unemotional Sadie. 'Plenty of tears to be shed in this old life without shedding them when you're happy! Come along, honey; tell us what the old boy said.'

I dried my eyes, and became a little more composed.

'He said I'd done a most deceitful and rep-rep something or other.'

'Reprehensible, you mean?' said Isobel, who always knew the meaning of long words.

148

I nodded.

'Yes – and he said I'd created a pres- pres—'

'Precedent,' put in Isobel helpfully.

'A precedent in wriggling into Sadler's Wells School under somebody else's name,' I went on, 'and that I deserved to be sent home in disgrace.'

'Well?' said a chorus of awestruck voices.

'He said that that was what I *deserved*, but that you don't always get what you deserve – especially in a ballet school. He said he wasn't going to turn me out because he saw how very much I loved dancing, and that as a matter of fact I was quite promising. Yes, he really said that,' I repeated dreamily. ' "Quite promising." '

'Gosh! Did he really?' said Janet with a whistle. 'Imagine it? The Director!'

'Then he asked me if I really *wanted* to go into the ballet; if I thought I could put up with all the hard work, and the discipline you have to submit to if you're going to be a dancer – no late nights at parties, exercising every morning, rehearsals, thinking of nothing but ballet all the time.'

'And what did you say?' asked Sadie with glowing eyes. '*I'd* have said *yes*!'

'So did I,' I told her. 'I said that dancing – even exercises – wasn't like work, not after riding and looking after my pony. I told him about Mummy expecting me to be a vet, and how Nigel – he's my cousin – said that I positively *cringed* every time a horse so much as swished his tail, and I asked him – the Director, I mean – if he thought it was much use my being a vet if I cringed every time a horse swished his tail, and he laughed and said no, he didn't think it was! Then he sat looking at me with his dark eyes – you know the way he does, as if he saw things

149

beyond you – and then he said I could go back to my class. But of course the class is over now – it's nearly lunchtime. Never mind I'll be able to go to Serge's Character class this afternoon.'

'So you'll be staying on?' asked Isobel. 'What about the real Mariella?'

'Oh, I forgot to tell you,' I answered, struggling out of my tunic, and pulling a dress on over my tights so as to look decent for lunch, 'Mariella is to have her audition next week – he promised that the awful thing *I'd* done wouldn't spoil her chances. Not that she really wants her chance, but I suppose her mother wants her to. And – oh, most important – the Director said that he's going north tomorrow to give a series of lectures in various towns, and one of them is Newcastle! That's near where I live. He said that while he's there he's going to look up my parents and explain and see what can be done about me. Well, you know what that means? When the Director says he'll see about anything, it's as good as done!'

'Gosh, yes, you're right!' exclaimed Janet.

'Oh, and I've just remembered something else – the Director said I must go straight away and apologize to both Gilbert and Lady Bailey.'

'Well, Lady Bailey's gone home – I saw her with my own eyes,' Sadie said. 'She drove off in an outsize car with a chauffeur positively *coated* in gold braid and buttons!'

'I'll just have to write to her then,' I said. 'Poor old thing! I threw my ballet shoes at her.'

'You *didn't*!'

'Yes, I did. At least I threw them at her feet. It was terrible of me, and she's such a nice old thing, too.'

'I seem to think I heard you call her a revolting old hag

150

not so long ago?' said Janet with a smile.

'Did I? I must have been all het-up. She's not a hag at all. She's a dear, and I must have given her a *dreadful* impression of the Sadler's Wells Ballet School.'

'Well, Gilbert's still in the Baylis Hall,' volunteered Sadie. 'He's talking to Miss Best about the music for something or other. You'll just catch him if you're quick. Go on – there's only three minutes before lunch.'

I dashed back to the Baylis Hall for the third time that morning. As Sadie had said, Gilbert was still there, deep in conversation with Miss Best, the pianist.

'Please, Mr Delahaye – I've come to apologize,' I said in a very meek voice.

Gilbert looked up.

'Oh, you have, have you?' he remarked, and by the tone of his voice, and the half-smile on his face, I gathered that he wasn't really so very furious. I have a shrewd idea that I'd only done what he'd have liked to do himself!

'Yes,' I said. 'I'm really most awfully sorry to have been so rude.'

'Um,' said Gilbert, making me a funny little mock bow. 'Well, if it's not too much to ask – who exactly are you? I gathered from your own lips that you aren't Mariella Foster.'

'I'm Jane,' I said.

'I gathered that too,' said Gilbert with a smile. 'You told us so – several times! But Jane *who*?'

'Jane Foster. I'm Mariella's cousin.'

'Ah, now I begin to see daylight,' Gilbert said with a shrug. 'But only just! Well, Jane, you'd better remove your ballet shoes from the floor before the next class trips over them! And another time, make sure the rightful

151

owner of your *nom de plume* hasn't got any childhood friends in the offing when you do your impersonating act. It's apt to be embarrassing to all concerned! And by the way, Jane,' he added as I was beating a hasty retreat, 'I liked your interpretation of the Dance of the Sugar Plum Fairy. Where did you learn it? And what were you thinking about when you were doing it?'

'I learnt it at Madame Viret's studio where Mariella has her dancing lessons,' I said. 'In Maestro Stcherbakof's class.' I didn't answer the second part of his question. After all, a dancer's thoughts are her own secret, aren't they?

Chapter 9

In the Dressing-room

ALTHOUGH, as I said before, Gloria Higgins had never been a friend of mine, she suddenly seemed to take a tremendous interest in me. I expect it was idle curiosity, really.

'So you live in the wilds of Scotland, Mariella? – So sorry! I should say Jane, shouldn't I?' she said on the afternoon after the Lady Bailey affair. We had just come out of Character class, and were getting ready to go home.

'Not quite!' I laughed. 'I live in Northumberland – in the country.'

'Do you live in a big house?' she persisted, combing her hair out of its neat roll, and pinning it into glamorous curls on the top of her head. 'How many rooms are there?'

I considered for a while.

'I really don't know,' I said at length. 'I've never counted them.'

'Gosh!' Gloria seemed awestruck. 'It *must* be big – not to know how many rooms there are. And I suppose you have goodness knows how many servants?'

'Only three,' I said.

'Only three? And I suppose you have a gardener, and a chauffeur, and a groom, and a gamekeeper?'

I didn't detect the sarcasm in her voice.

'No, not a gamekeeper,' I said.

'No gamekeeper? Oh, *really*,' drawled Gloria. 'You *must* be badly off! And I suppose you have a horse to ride?'

'A pony,' I corrected. 'As a matter of fact, I have two.' I was about to explain about Dapple being too stolid for me in Mummy's opinion, and about Firefly being my birthday present, but Gloria broke in:

'Well, if you've got all that, why on earth did you want to come *here*?' She glanced round the bare dressing-room. 'You must have a tile off!'

'I came here because I wanted to learn to dance,' I said, nettled at her tone. 'And Sadler's Wells is the best school – bar none! Why did you come here yourself?'

'Me?' Gloria repeated. 'I'll tell you, my innocent, shall I? I live in what is known as the East End – in a tene-ment. We have two rooms, and there are eight of us – Mum and Dad, and six kids. I'm the eldest. If I didn't do this' – she flexed her shapely legs – 'I'd be doling out pounds of margarine in the shop round the corner, or scrubbing out people's offices – like Mum. I've got no brains, see – except in my legs! My reason for being here is purely mercenary, I assure you!'

'But doesn't it cost a lot?' I said.

'Only the fees,' said Gloria. 'My mum pays for them by charring. Quite the devoted ma, is my mum! She's like you; she's romantic – that's why she called me Gloria. Thinks she'll see her daughter wearing a mink coat and pearls! I live at home, see? Besides, I've been in pantomime before I came here, and that's well paid, if you like! I saved a tidy bit. But don't think I cherish any illusions of being chosen for the Company, and appearing at Covent Garden. But after being trained here it's easy to get a job elsewhere – even if it's only in musicals.'

'Don't be bitter, Gloria!' put in Scottish Janet.

'I'm not being bitter,' laughed Gloria. 'I'm a realist! *Everyone* can't be chosen for the Company. Otherwise it wouldn't be the first-class company it is. It would be full of people like *me*.' She laughed again – a strained, unnatural laugh. 'No. Any minute I'm expecting to be sent for by the Director and told – ever so sweetly and politely – that I've been here too long, and it's time I gave someone else a chance. Someone really promising – like you, Mariella. I mean Jane!'

'Well, what do you expect them to do?' put in Janet. 'Keep you here for ever? Because you know, Gloria, you *aren't* good enough for the Company. And surely you'd rather be told gently than any other way. Besides, if you let him, the Director will always help you to find a job.'

Gloria didn't answer. I don't think she had heard a word of what Janet was saying.

'If you ask me,' she went on, 'we're just a lot of poor moths fluttering round a candle, waiting for our wings to be singed! Well, I can understand most of us – we're just trying to get away from our drab lot, but you, Jane Foster – if that's your real name – well, I just *can't* understand why you don't stay safely at home in your big house and enjoy yourself.'

'I've told you – I want to dance,' I said simply.

Gloria shrugged her shoulders expressively.

'So do we all. I wasn't telling the truth just now when I said my reason for being here was purely mercenary. I'm like all the rest – I dream dreams about dancing leading roles at Covent Garden, like Margot Fonteyn; or being a wonderful, fairy-tale princess, like Moira Shearer; or an exquisite Lilac Fairy, like Veronica Weston. Sometimes,' she added fiercely, 'I wish I'd never heard the name of ballet! I wish I'd gone behind a counter, selling hunks ot cheese, and being called "Glor" by the grocer's assistant!'

'Look here,' put in Sadie, 'I don't know who started all this. I don't know why you should all start getting dramatic just because Mariella has turned out to be Jane, and the Director hasn't expelled her. It seems to me this ought to be a moment of rejoicing – not – not—'

'Solemn premonition,' Gloria said with a laugh. 'Well, Jane – don't say you haven't been warned!'

Then, just as she said the words, the door opened, and the impersonal voice of the Director's secretary said:

'Gloria Higgins! The Director wants to see you in his office.'

There was a horrified silence. Gloria herself turned as white as a sheet.

'My hour has come!' she said dramatically. 'Oh, well – in some ways it'll be a relief to know the worst!' She put more lipstick on her already too-red lips, flicked some powder on her nose, and walked to the door. With her hand on the knob, she turned.

'We who are about to die salute you!' she said tragically. Then she shut the door behind her.

When she had gone, I asked:

'What on earth did she mean?'

'It was what the Roman gladiators used to say when they fought,' explained Janet. 'We did that last term in ancient history at the Continuation classes. She meant she was going to be turned out.'

'Perhaps it's not that at all,' I said, thinking of the happy ending to my own interview. 'Perhaps it's something altogether different.'

Janet shook her curly head.

'No. We all knew Gloria would have to go sooner or later. She hasn't improved much since she came, you know, and that's more than a year ago. They've given her every chance, but sometimes I think she's not even as good as she was. And besides, she's terribly "mannered" – perhaps it's with being in pantomime so much when she was young.'

'It seems hard,' I said with a sigh.

'I know it does,' Janet admitted, 'but it's the fortunes of war. It's the same in anything competitive. There's not room for *everyone* at the top.'

We sat on the benches, silent. Nobody seemed in a hurry to get dressed. In a very few minutes Gloria was back. She was still white, and you could see the unshed tears in her eyes, but she held her head high.

'European Ballet Company for yours truly!' she said with a strange, forced laugh.

'What did he say?' demanded Janet.

'Oh, the usual things?' said Gloria. 'He was all sympathy and sorrow. Poor man – he has an awful job telling all us moths to go and flutter elsewhere! He was very helpful, really.'

'But, Gloria,' put in Sadie, 'you can't go into a third-rate company like the European. You *can't*!'

'I'm only a third-rate person myself,' Gloria answered soberly. 'Anyway, it's either that or a musical, and I'd rather be in ballet proper, in spite of what I said a bit ago. It's either purse or pride, if you see what I mean. I'd rather be in the European Ballet than, say, *Dance for Poppa*, even if the latter *is* better paid. I'll get a splendid opportunity of seeing the capitals of Europe, even if my digs are up among the roofs of Paris, or down among

157

the slums of Moscow – if they have any slums in Moscow!'

'But you're not going *now*?' I said, wide-eyed.

'Yes. Why not? What's there to stay for? I may as well get started earning my own living. I've been feeling for a bit that I've lived on Mum long enough. It's time she had a let-up on the charring.' She crammed her hat down over her curls, shrugged on her coat, pushed several ancient pairs of ballet shoes into a dilapidated attaché-case, and walked to the door again.

'Well, so long!' she said. 'Good luck, all you poor moths!' With that she was gone out of our lives for ever.

There was a long silence after this, during which we all thought our own thoughts. Janet broke in.

'Och! We mustn't get all hot and bothered about Gloria,' she said in her soft, Scottish voice. 'If she isn't good enough for the Company, she isn't, and that's that!'

'She's right, though,' Isobel said soberly. 'We *are* a lot of moths fluttering round the limelight. Most of us will get singed, but one or two will survive. Don't look so down in the mouth, Mariella – beg pardon, I should say, Jane! I have an idea that you'll be one of them. You've got a "look" about you, and when a dancer's got that look, it means you'll see them dancing leading roles sooner or later. I expect the Director saw it too. He's a shrewd old boy!'

'There's one other reason why Jane's sure to go to the top,' remarked Sadie. 'She doesn't *have* to dance, and when one doesn't have to do a thing, one always does it especially well. Have you noticed?'

'I've noticed something else, too,' put in Isobel. 'It's after half past four. Are you lot going to stop here all day discussing Gloria Higgins and her misfortunes?'

'We weren't,' contradicted Sadie. 'We were just saying—'

'Oh, come on!' begged Isobel. 'I'm so hungry after that Character class I could eat a horse!'

Chapter 10

The Wonderful Idea

WHAT shall I say about my first real week at the Wells? I say 'real' because until now I had merely been a masquerader. Now I was there in my own right. I was filled with joy and excitement and – yes, apprehension. For who knew what the next few days might bring? Each morning, when I arrived at the school, I wondered whether the dreaded telegram had arrived from Mummy and Daddy, forbidding me to continue my dancing career. Each morning I wondered whether today would be my last, for, I had to admit it, I *had* been a little high-handed in the way I had gone about things. The fact that it had been Mariella who had thought of the plan in the first place, and had egged me on to its accomplishment, was no excuse. I had fallen in with it only too readily!

But time went on, and still the telegram didn't come. I knew that the Director had left for his tour of the north, and that most probably by now he'd have seen my parents. I had carefully not mentioned anything about Sadler's Wells in my letters home, because I felt that the Director would break the tidings a great deal more diplomatically than I should.

As for Mariella – she took the news of my unmasking quite calmly.

'Oh, I always knew you'd be found out sooner or later,' she announced.

'But, Mariella,' I expostulated, 'I thought you said—'

'Oh, I expect I said all sorts of stupid things!' she laughed. 'After all, I had to do *something* to stop you having the jitters, Jane! But I knew all the time that the whole thing was impossible, and that someone who knew me would be bound to turn up, or the Director's secretary would send Daddy a letter tearing the whole thing to ribbons, or something.'

'Then why—'

'Well, I thought that by then you'd have got a footing in the school,' went on Mariella. 'And you must admit,' she added triumphantly, 'that I was right!'

'Y-yes,' I admitted doubtfully, 'but—'

'But me no buts!' exclaimed Mariella. 'Let's go and break the glad news to Daddy, and see if he's as much a philosopher as I think he is.'

I wasn't quite sure what a philosopher was, but I didn't like to show my ignorance by asking, so I obediently followed Mariella to the library where Uncle Oscar was working. Watching the arrogant tilt of her red-gold head, I thought how marvellous it must feel to be as cocksure and confident of oneself as Mariella was!

'Oh, Daddy!' she announced, perching herself on his table and swinging her legs. 'I've got a most awful blow for you! It's *Jane* who's going to go to Sadler's Wells to be a dancer – not me. In fact, she's already gone!' In a few short sentences, she told him about the audition and everything that had happened since.

Uncle Oscar slowly withdrew his head from the inevitable showcase, and studied his daughter thoughtfully.

'I suspected as much!' he announced. 'At least, I had no idea about Jane's aspirations, or that you'd taken matters into your own hands quite so completely about Sadler's Wells, but I've often suspected that we were mistaken in our chosen career for you, Mariella. I think your mother realizes it, too.'

'Oh, Daddy – then we *can* change places, can't we?' shrieked Mariella wildly, jumping off the table and clasping her father round the neck.

'Change places?' Uncle Oscar echoed, taking off his glasses, wiping them, and then putting them on again. 'You go a little too fast for me, my dear. Change places with whom?'

'With Jane, of course,' said Mariella. 'Don't you *see*? She's doing what I want to do, and I'm supposed to be doing what she wants to do. It's so *simple*! All you have to do is to send the Director a wire – a nice long one. You *do* know the Director, Daddy? Yes, I thought you did. Well, he'll listen to *you* – everyone does. You must say that if he can arrange for Jane to come here to the Wells, *I'll* go up there to Monks Hollow to keep Aunt Carol and Uncle Harold company. It's awfully lonely for me here, Daddy, with Mummy nearly always away, and you—'

'I understand,' said Uncle Oscar quietly, and, I thought, a little sadly.

'Oh, Daddy, I didn't mean that – truly I didn't,' exclaimed Mariella, suddenly conscience-stricken. 'But you know you *are* a little apt to forget people are there – especially when you're writing a book, or cataloguing things, and it's a fact, you don't know the least thing about horses.'

'No, thank heavens!' said Uncle Oscar fervently. 'There's nothing I detest more than horses!'

'And there's nothing *I* love more!' exclaimed Mariella passionately. 'I – I think I could *live* in a stable! Oh, Daddy – you simply must manage it somehow. You *will*

162

send the wire to the Director, won't you, and another one to Mummy breaking the wonderful news to her? Do you realize – she doesn't know yet?'

'It *had* occurred to me,' murmured Uncle Oscar, carefully lifting a small, pale green object like a little bar of soap out of the cabinet, and examining it carefully through his magnifying glass. 'Most interesting! *Most* interesting! In fact, unique!'

'Now, Daddy – you're forgetting me again,' said Mariella accusingly.

'Er – what's that, my dear?'

'The telegrams, darling!' prompted Mariella. 'The *telegrams*! Two of them. One for the Director, and the other – a cable – for Mummy. You *will* send them?'

'A cablegram will cost a lot of money,' expostulated Uncle Oscar.

'Well, what if it does!' said Mariella offhandedly. 'You've got loads of cash, and think of poor Mummy and all the anxiety it's going to save her. Promise, Daddy!'

'Very well, my dear, if it will make you happy.'

'Happy!' shrieked Mariella. 'Happy! Why, I could jump over Nelson's Column! Jane, do you know what it is? It's a real *pas de deux*! That's a dance for two people, you know. You and me! Yes, it's our *pas de deux*!'

A short time later I wrote a letter to Miss Martin, the principal of my Newcastle dancing school.

> 140a Fortnum Mansions,
> London, W1.

Dear Miss Martin,

I expect Daddy will have told you about the awful thing I did while I was staying here, and how it has all ended happily. But just in case he hasn't, this is what happened.

You see, Mariella – she's the cousin I told you about, remember? – well, her mother, Aunt Irma, is the world-famous Irma Foster, and she'd got an audition fixed for Mariella for Sadler's Wells School. Well, Mariella didn't want to go to it one little bit, so I went in her place because our initials are the same, and I'm so frightfully keen on dancing. It seemed all right at the time like a lot of naughty things you do, but the Director said it was most reprehensible, and a precedent, so now I know how awful it really was!

The audition was wonderful, and I got into the school, and had three glorious weeks until the DIS-COVERY! I shall never forget that frightful day – not if I live to be a hundred! I shall never forget shouting: 'I'm Jane! Jane! JANE!' and Lady Bailey with her mouth open like a fish, and poor Gilbert looking so astonished, and, last but not least, seeing the sphinx-like figure of the DIRECTOR sitting like Fate up in the balcony! Gilbert, by the way, is Mr Delahaye, and he's the most wonderful teacher you can imagine, but he has a TEMPER, and is apt to be sarcastic. For instance, I heard him telling Lady Bailey that I was temperamental – all because I threw my ballet shoes at her! You'll be relieved to hear that I apologized in dust and ashes afterwards.

You don't know how wonderful it is to be a member of the Sadler's Wells Ballet School. You see, it's quite the most famous ballet school in the world – in spite of what Serge says about the Leningrad one – and you feel as proud as a peacock just to belong to it. But please don't ever think that I shall forget *you*, Miss

Martin. The last three years have been the happiest of my life – all through you! I shall never forget the very first time Daddy brought me to your studio – all the lights reflecting in the mirrors, and you being so kind, and showing me everything so patiently. When I come home for the holidays, I shall ask for permission to come back and practise with you. You have to get permission because they don't like you going to other schools in the holidays in case you get the styles mixed up, which is quite right when you come to think of it. But Gilbert – Mr Delahaye – says you are one of the finest dancing teachers he knows, and I can tell you that he's met most of the famous ones!

The Director worked miracles when he came to Newcastle and saw Mummy and Daddy. He not only convinced them that dancing is my *métier* (I've just looked this word up in the dictionary) but he put a wonderful idea into their heads about having Mariella to live at Monks Hollow in my place, so that she can learn to be a vet. Of course, it was Mariella's idea in the first place, but they don't know that. Mariella would make a marvellous vet; *she* doesn't mind a bit when a horse swishes his tail, or shows the whites of his eyes. In fact, she says she likes it! If Aunt Irma agrees to this plan, Mariella would live in Northumberland during term-time and go to my day school in Newcastle, and then come back to London in the holidays, and I'd do vice versa, if you see what I mean. I've just looked up vice versa in the dictionary, too! Then Mariella would follow in Mummy's footsteps – I should say, hoofprints, really! – with the horses, and I'd follow Aunt Irma's at the Wells. Of course Aunt Irma is away in New Zealand at present so we can't discuss

it with her, but I think she'll agree to our plan, because
Mariella had her audition for the Wells School the day
before yesterday – and they turned her down on
account of her thighs – they're too big, I mean, so it
looks like Fate, doesn't it? If I hadn't gatecrashed
there wouldn't have been a single member of the family at the Wells! Think of that! Uncle Oscar says he
doesn't think Fate had a great deal to do with it. I don't
know what he means.

I could write lots more about our classes, and how
funny Carmencita is in the RAD classes, doing all the
strictly academical exercises with a Spanish wriggle
and how Timothy – one of the male students – played
Romeo and Juliet in the Baylis Hall, and tried to climb
up into the gallery where I was sitting – I was Juliet, of
course. Well, just as he had got nearly to the top, in
walked Miss Smailes – she's on the strict side – and
said '*Timothy!*' in such a scandalized voice that poor
Timothy came down quicker than he intended and
nearly landed on top of her! Then there's Janet, my
best friend. She's got a real dancing part in the Faren-
dole in *The Sleeping Beauty*, and she's a Rat, too. And
Sadie, and Isobel, and June, and Lilian – they're all
special friends of mine – they're all in a ballet they're
doing down at the Sadler's Wells Theatre, and they
think they'll be in the Company soon. Well, as I say, I
could write lots more, but this is a very long letter as it
is, so I think I'd better stop now.

With much love from your affectionate pupil,
JANE MONKHOUSE FOSTER, MSWS

(The letters after my name mean – Member of the
Sadler's Wells School.)

PS – I've nearly forgotten the most important thing of all. A list went up on the Winter Garden notice-board, and I'm down for a part in *The Sleeping Beauty* – several parts, in fact! I'm to be a Mouse, and a Page as well! Think of it – at Covent Garden Theatre! My stage career has already begun! I shall be dancing on the self-same boards as Margot Fonteyn and Veronica Weston. And to think that only three years ago I'd never even heard of them!

JANE

Part Three

Pas de Deux
Written by Mariella

Chapter 1

The Years Between

I'M Mariella, and of course you've heard quite a lot about me. I'm really rather important, because, if it hadn't been for me, Jane would never have gone to Sadler's Wells, at all, and become famous.

Jane says it's all very well to write your life story, but it's terribly difficult to write about your own success. I don't see this at all, but I must admit that it's exactly like Jane. She's so modest! When I asked her how people were going to know how she got on at the school, and how she got her CHANCE at last, she just said: 'Well, I expect they just *won't* know – unless *you* finish the story, Mariella.' Now I must say that, for Jane, this was nothing short of a brainwave, so, if you don't mind awfully having a change of authorship, I'll carry on the good work, and tell you what happened to us when we changed places.

At first Jane went along slowly at the school. She got lots of small parts in the ballets – especially in *The Sleeping Beauty*, because they're always wanting small people for that particular ballet – Rats, and Mice, and Pages, and so on. After about two years' hard work, she got into the

Opera Ballet; then went on tour with the Theatre Ballet – or Second Company, as it is often called. Finally, she got into the principal company at Covent Garden.

Well, now we are both eighteen, and today I had a letter from Jane.

140a Fortnum Mansions,
London, W1.

Dear Mariella,

I'm awfully sorry to have been so long in answering your last letter, but really you have no idea how terribly busy I've been. I'm writing this in the dressing-room between acts, as it is positively the only spare minute I have. Nothing very exciting has happened lately – just the ordinary routine. I've danced quite a few interesting roles – the Lilac Fairy in *Sleeping Beauty*; one of the Miseries in *Sylphides*. They're the leaders of the *corps de ballet*, you know. But of course you do! When we went on tour to one or two big towns I danced one of the solos in *Sylphides*. It was called the Prélude. I also did the Odette solo out of *Lac des Cygnes*. At present I'm doing Myrtha, Queen of the Wilis, in *Giselle*, and I've just got the classical *pas de deux* in *Les Patineurs* – the Girl in White. I love it, because your mother used to do it, remember? You've got a wonderful mother, you know, Mariella! I am also understudying Veronica Weston in *The Sleeping Beauty*. Veronica is the most wonderful dancer you ever saw. She's so satisfying to watch, and she makes everything look so easy. All the time she's dancing you feel that she's living in another world. Every night she's on, I stand in the wings and watch her. Apart from being her understudy, I love watching her.

170

I have danced the Lilac Fairy in The Sleeping Beauty

Are you really all coming to London next month as you said in your last letter? If so, why not make it Sept 8th to the 15th? Then you'll see Veronica in the gala performance of *The Sleeping Beauty*. They *say* royalty will be there! If you will let me know how many of you will be coming, I will book seats for you. Two nights during that week they're doing *The Gods go A-Begging* – Ninette de Valois' ballet, you know. I shall be the Serving-maid in this. Perhaps I could book seats for you for two nights – one to see Veronica, and the other to see me – if you're really sure you *want* to see me!

I must tell you the awful nightmare I had last night. I dreamt that I was a poor, sad-coloured moth, fluttering about in the wings of Covent Garden Theatre. Try as I would, I couldn't find my way on to the stage. Always I was cut off by some lofty piece of scenery, and from behind the scenery would step a huge candle ready to burn me up! At last, however, I did manage to get on to the stage. The orchestra was there, and the conductor standing ready with his baton poised. I could see the gleam of white shirt-fronts in the darkened auditorium, and the sparkle of jewels in the boxes as I waited. Then I began to dance the Dance of the Sugar Plum Fairy from *Le Casse Noisette*.

All went well until the very end when I was making my curtsies to the audience. Then a terrible and frightening thing happened. The conductor – it was the famous Sebastian Scott – suddenly turned into an enormous candle. His mouth took on a more ironic twist than usual, and he yelled at me: 'You did that all wrong! Your interpretation is the worst I've ever seen!' Then his face changed and became that of

172

Gilbert Delahaye saying: 'Flik-flak in the centre, please! You see, Lady Bailey, ballet training isn't always so very graceful!' Then all the people in the theatre stood up, and began to hiss and boo.

I woke up with a start to find myself fighting with the bedclothes and yelling: 'I *didn't* do it all wrong! My interpretation was perfect. It was! It was!'

Well, they say dreams go by opposites, so that one ought to be a good omen for my dancing career!

I think I have told you all my news. I must dash now and make up my face. Please write soon and tell me how things are going with you.

Love,

JANE

I answered this letter by return, and I think perhaps you would like to see it.

Monks Hollow,
Nr Bychester,
Northumberland.

Dear Jane,

Many thanks for your letter. I am so glad that you are doing so well. Yes, we shall be coming up to see you dance next month, and Aunt Carol says the dates you mention will do nicely, so please book the seats as you suggested. I shall be glad to see Veronica Weston again, though of course it's *you*, Jane, we're all dying to see – naturally! Although I hate dancing myself, I love to see other people doing it! I expect it's because I'm so dreadfully lazy!

You ask how things are with me. Everything is going swimmingly, thank you! I got my Higher School

Certificate all right, and am beginning my training – veterinary surgeon – at the Michaelmas term. Nigel says he never heard of anything so ridiculous. He says the training is far too long and expensive for a girl! I don't think Nigel approves of careers for women – he's old-fashioned! He says it's just a waste of time, anyway, in my case, because I shall be sure to go and get married in the middle of it! When I asked him who he had in mind for me to marry, he said he *had* someone in mind, but he wasn't telling me who! He's as much a tease as ever, is Nigel!

Wasn't our *pas de deux* a wonderful idea, Jane? You can't imagine how much I've enjoyed my three years up here in your beautiful home, and judging by your letters, *you* seem to have had fun in London – despite the hard work. I never seem to work at all here, because you can't call mucking out stables and grooming horses work, can you? Not like all those awful *développés*, and *battements*, and things!

This next remark may sound conceited, but I really ride rather well now. I won the Adjacent Hunts Ladies' Race at the Tyndale Point-to-Point last March, and I've got quite an array of silver cups and trophies on the mantelpiece in my bedroom that I've won at local gymkhanas. Nigel says I've got almost as many as he has, which is something, because he had quite a few years' start of me! By the way, Nigel won the Members' Race at the Hayden Point-to-Point, and the Members' and Farmers' at the Braes of Derwent.

Aunt Carol has just come in and read my letter, and she says will you only book *three* seats for *The Sleeping Beauty* performance. She says she can stand a whole ballet performance to see her daughter dance, but not otherwise, so it will only be Uncle Harold, Nigel, and me. I don't know what Nigel will think of it all; I don't believe he's ever been to the ballet! Of course you know that Nigel has decided to be an estate agent, and he starts as a pupil with Mr Forster next month. He's nineteen now, and ever so grown-up. You'll really have to find time to come up north before long, you know, Jane, or you'll have forgotten Monks Hollow altogether! It seems ages since you were here.

You should see my new hunter. Her name is Jasmine Flower – Jas for short! Isn't it lovely the way one can give horses the most outlandish names, and no one thinks it's funny?

Well, here's to seeing you in London on the 8th!

Lots of love from your affectionate

MARIELLA

Chapter 2

To See Jane Dance!

WE caught the Pullman express that leaves Newcastle in the early afternoon, and after we had left the city behind, I pulled a letter out of my handbag – the letter I had received from Jane only that morning. I'd hardly had time to read it properly yet.

'What does she say?' asked Nigel curiously. He was sitting on the double seat beside me, and Aunt Carol and Uncle Harold were on the seat opposite.

'It's quite an interesting letter,' I answered. 'All about Veronica Weston. She's had flu, and been dreadfully ill. Jane says that Sebastian Scott – the conductor – has been nearly frantic with anxiety. Veronica is engaged to him, you know. Every day, while she's been so ill, he's sent her a basket of red roses. Gosh! It must have cost him a fortune! But of course, as Jane says, he has loads of money. She says that not long ago, he bought back the family estates, and he and Veronica are going there for their honeymoon. They're being married in a few weeks' time.'

'What else does she say?' asked Uncle Harold. 'Anything about her dancing?'

'Oh, yes – lots! She says that last week, when Veronica was so ill, she – Jane, I mean – danced her role as the Princess Aurora in *The Sleeping Beauty* at the rehearsals, and at the dress rehearsal Madame herself – the director of the Company – was there, and Jane says she talked to her afterwards for ages, and was ever so sweet!'

After this we were all silent for quite a long time. I sat looking out of the wide window at the scenery flying past – at the smoky town of Gateshead, and the industrial villages of the Tyneside, and then at Durham Cathedral, standing on its rocky promontory, overlooking the River Wear. Finally I stole a glance at Nigel, sitting beside me. He had grown very big and tall, had Nigel. His unruly shock of tow-coloured hair was now cut short, and brushed into order, though it still did its best to curl! His features were strong and cleanly cut; his complexion still ruddy. He looked rather as if he were 'The Boy David', stepped out of the pages of my Bible story-book!

I gave a little sigh. Did Nigel, I wondered, know just how good-looking he was? Did he realize that, everywhere he went, girls looked at him with open admiration? I thought he did!

We had tea on the train, and in the early evening, we arrived at King's Cross. Mummy and Daddy were there to meet us, Daddy looking as dreamy and absent-minded as ever. I expect he was thinking about the gala performance of *The Sleeping Beauty* tomorrow night, and wondering how on earth he was going to find something new to say about it! If only he'd known the astonishing thing that was going to happen, he'd have looked much more wide awake! But of course none of us knew that then!

Mummy was wearing black – she nearly always does – and the usual pair of little buttoned boots she had specially made for her, and which she says keeps her ankles slim. I don't believe they do, really, but there's no denying the fact – Mummy's ankles aren't any bigger than most people's wrists!

177

We took a taxi straight to the flat, dropping Nigel and Uncle Harold at the Hotel Rubens – which is directly opposite Buckingham Palace – on our way, because there wasn't room for them at 140a Fortnum Mansions.

We went up to the fourth floor in the lift, and when we opened the door of the lobby, I couldn't help feeling how small and neat, and like a dolls' house it was! I was to share Jane's bedroom, Mummy said, so I went in there to take off my things. The room had once been mine, of course, but it didn't seem nearly as much mine as the room I had left at Monks Hollow with the row of silver trophies on the mantelpiece. There wasn't a mantelpiece in this room – at least not one that would hold silver cups. The narrow cream shelf with its chromium edge merely held one blown-glass ornament with a large photograph of Jane above – Jane in *Sylphides* costume. There were more lovely photographs of Jane on the dressing-table with its sunk centre, and there was one of me standing beside Firefly. It must have been taken ages ago, before I grew too big to ride him.

I stared at myself critically in the triple mirrors. Yes, I wasn't bad-looking, all things considered. My red-gold curls were cut very short, which made me look startlingly like Aunt Carol. With the light behind me, I looked a cross between a boy and a cherub! But the thing I noticed most was the fact that I looked years and years older than Jane, if you could judge by her photograph which was evidently a recent one as it had the date scrawled across the bottom corner. She was dressed as Odette in *Lac des Cygnes*, and her smooth, oval face, with its big, dark eyes, looked about fifteen!

I was just thinking how attractive Jane had become – you couldn't call it pretty, exactly – when Mummy came in and said that dinner was ready, and would I please come quickly before it got cold. She added that it was already quite cold enough before it got to us!

'Oh, and by the way – Jane asked me to apologize for her. She hadn't time between rehearsal and tonight's performance to meet you all at the station. She won't be home before eleven, I'm afraid.'

'Don't worry, Mummy!' I said. 'I didn't expect Jane to meet us. I know too much about the theatre for that!'

As a matter of fact, it was nearly half past eleven when Jane did get home, and after that of course we gossiped and gossiped, so that it was nearly one o'clock when we finally went to bed. And even then, we talked! It was mostly about the old days – that far-off summer when Mummy and I had gone to stay at Monks Hollow, and I'd met Nigel, and we'd all had such fun.

'Do you remember that old sheep that fell down the cliff at Housesteads, and how I climbed down to the ledge and hung on to it round the neck!' laughed Jane. 'I believe that was the one and only time Nigel had the least respect for me! By the way, how is Nigel?'

'In the pink!' I said. 'And when I come to think of it, it's true – literally! He's a member of two local hunts, you know.'

'Oh, I can see Nigel being MFH one of these fine days,' said Jane. 'Goodness! I don't know what on earth he'll think when he sees a theatrical dressing-room! Rather different to the gun-room at Bychester, with its sporting prints and dogs.' She laughed. 'You really *must* bring him round behind on Wednesday, Mariella. I'd adore him to see me in my make-up, especially the false eyelashes!'

179

'Oh, I'll bring him round all right,' I promised. 'It will be very good for him – show him how the other half of the world lives, and all that! Nigel is very sweet, but he *is* rather a dyed-in-the wool English country squire! By the way, what were you in tonight, Jane?'

'*Sylphides – pas de Trois.* Veronica Weston did the waltz. She still looks dreadfully ill, and really she had no business to be dancing at all tonight. Batty Scott thinks so, too – Sebastian Scott, you know – her fiancé.'

'Yes – you told me about him in your letter,' I said. 'But everyone has heard about Sebastian Scott, I should think. I do read about the arts, Jane, even if I don't practise them!'

'Sorry!' apologized Jane. 'I keep forgetting you're Aunt Irma's daughter. You don't look a bit like the daughter of a world-famous ballerina, you know, Mariella!'

'Oh, well, as long as *you* do – that's all that matters!' I laughed. 'There's at least *someone* to follow in poor Mummy's footsteps! And what about tomorrow night? Is Veronica Weston dancing the Princess Aurora?'

'Oh, yes! It's the gala performance, and of course she feels she must do it. I can see her point, naturally, but I do think she ought to have given tonight a miss. But you know what Veronica is – her art is all in all to her. Batty Scott was furious! There was such a row in Veronica's dressing-room after the performance – they had a real, slap-up quarrel! Of course they're always quarrelling. It doesn't mean a thing. Only at the time you'd think it was life and death! Veronica was as white as a sheet, and Batty as black as a thundercloud. He's got those very dark blue eyes that go black when he's angry, and spit fire! Well, the two of them argued and argued about whether

180

Veronica ought or ought not to go on tomorrow night, and in the end, Veronica threw Batty's roses on the floor at his feet. Then Batty said that this time he was through! He had a good mind to chuck the gala performance! He had a good mind to chuck everything!'

'My goodness!' I exclaimed. 'Do you think he will, Jane?'

'Not a bit of it,' Jane said tranquilly. 'Of course he'll conduct at the gala performance. He's under contract, for one thing – not that that would weigh with Batty if he'd made up his mind – but he's far too conscientious to let the management down at the last moment. He's like Veronica – his art comes first every time. Oh, yes – he was only being temperamental.'

'Then what happened?' I asked.

'Well, Veronica took off her engagement ring and flung it down on top of the roses. Whereupon Batty ground his heel into the lot and stalked out, banging the door so hard you could hear it halfway down the Strand! Then Veronica burst into tears, and wept for quite five minutes on the shoulder of her dresser. Poor old Gladys kept patting her on the head like a dog and saying "There! There! Don't take on so, dearie! He'll come back again, never fear!" ... "I don't *want* him to come back!" sobbed Veronica. "I don't ever want to see him again! I hate him."'

'What a thrilling row!' I said. 'No wonder you were late, Jane!'

'Yes, it *was* rather thrilling,' Jane agreed with a yawn. 'Goodness, I'm sleepy! I wonder whether *all* grown-up people behave like that, Mariella?'

'Well, *you're* grown up, aren't you?' I laughed. 'You're eighteen, though goodness knows you don't look it! No,

I don't think ordinary people do behave like that — just *prima ballerinas*, and opera singers, and famous concert pianists, and suchlike phenomena! After all, the public likes them to be temperamental. It's picturesque! But wouldn't it amaze people if *I* suddenly turned temperamental, Jane! Supposing I went to the meet of the hounds, flung my bowler at the master's feet, and yelled at him: "This is the last time your mouldy hunt shall see my face!" or something to that effect, wouldn't he get a shock!'

Jane giggled.

'Yes, it *would* sound funny! Oh, well, I expect Veronica will have got over her tantrum by tomorrow night, and will dance the Princess Aurora with a dreamy smile on her face, and the most incredible *arabesque*, while Scott conducts the augmented symphony orchestra, looking like a tiger on the leash, and sparks coming out of his evening-dress suit! Then they'll make up their quarrel after the performance.' She yawned again. 'Well, Mariella — if you don't mind, I think I'll go to sleep. I've had rather a hard day, but then all my days are hard — even if they are happy. Goodnight, Mariella!'

Chapter 3

The Princess Awakes!

WHEN I arrived in London, I had thought how small and cramped the flat looked after the spacious rooms at Monks Hollow. Now, as Uncle Harold, Nigel, and I filed into the front row of the grand tier, I thought how big Covent Garden Theatre seemed to have grown in comparison with the provincial theatres I'd been in lately. The vast auditorium yawned in front of us like a great Roman amphitheatre. The orchestral pit and the stage seemed to be miles and miles away.

Jane came round from the stage to speak to us before the performance began. She told us that she would be watching in the wings, and promised to come and talk to us again in the first interval.

'Oh, look!' I exclaimed, seizing the programme that Uncle Harold held out. 'Look who's partnering Veronica Weston. It's Josef Linsk! He's Prince Florimund. You remember, Jane – we met him at the swimming baths ages and ages ago, and you fell for him!'

'Oh, Mariella – I *didn't*!' Jane said indignantly, turning pink. 'I only said he was a wonderful swimmer, and so he was. And of course it was a thrill meeting him.'

'You still think he's wonderful?' I persisted.

'I still think he's a wonderful dancer,' said Jane. 'And if you knew him, Mariella, you'd realize that he's not a bit conceited, really. He only makes people think he is because he's so like a child. When he does anything

183

especially brilliantly, he – well he *crows*!'

'Peter Pan, in fact!' I laughed. 'Well, I'm glad *I* haven't got to dance with him, anyway. Have *you* ever, Jane?'

Jane blushed again.

'Have I ever what? Oh, you mean have I ever danced with Josef. Only at rehearsals when I've taken Veronica Weston's place. And now I really *must* go. The orchestra is beginning the overture. Goodbye, Daddy! Goodbye, Nigel! See you in the interval, Mariella!'

She was gone, just as the first notes of Tchaikovsky's music filled the theatre.

'Who's that fellow in the orchestra?' Nigel wanted to know after a bit.

'Which one? Oh, you mean the conductor. Why, he's the famous Sebastian Scott. You know – Veronica Weston's fiancé. Would you like to have a look at him through the glasses? Uncle Harold's got them. Would you mind if we borrowed them for a minute, Uncle?' I passed the glasses over to Nigel. 'He's not exactly good-looking, is he, but there's something about him! He's what I call dynamic – like Maestro! Maestro is short for Ivan Dmitoritch Stcherbakof. He used to be my dancing master.'

'Good Lord!' Nigel said, passing over the glasses to me. 'What a name!'

'Yes, it is, isn't it?' I laughed. 'And he's just as dramatic as his name!'

Curiously I examined Sebastian Scott through the glasses. I had never seen him before, but I had read lots about him. Now, when I saw him in person for the first time, I couldn't help thinking how wonderful it was that this young man – for he *was* young; only in his twenties –

could control that huge, augmented orchestra with the smallest gesture of his sensitive hands. I had read about Sebastian Scott's wonderful hands, and now I realized just how wonderful they were. He wielded no baton and he used every inch of every finger to express his wishes – no, *commands* is a better word – using the orchestra as if it were a violin, and he a Yehudi Menuhin playing upon it!

The romantic story of the ballet unfolded itself in the prologue. King Florestan and his Queen arrived for the christening of their infant daughter, the Princess Aurora. The court made merry. The revels were interrupted dramatically by the arrival of the wicked fairy, Carabosse, with her attendant train of Rats and Mice. The spell was cast over the baby Princess, that she should die by pricking her finger with a spindle, and was mitigated by the timely arrival of the Lilac Fairy who decreed that she should fall into a deep sleep instead, until she should be awakened by a prince's kiss.

The years passed, and the first act opened on the lovely Princess Aurora's sixteenth birthday. Again all was gaiety and revel. Four princes arrived to ask for the Princess' hand in marriage. She danced with them all in turn, taking from each a rose, and when at last she fell to the ground, having pricked her finger with the fateful spindle, an audible sigh could be heard throughout the theatre. I sighed too! How beautifully she danced! She reminded me a little of Margot Fonteyn, yet of course she was quite different, for each ballerina is different; each invests the role with her own personality. As she lay upon the stage, apparently lifeless, panic seized me.

'Wouldn't it be awful,' I said aloud, 'wouldn't it be dreadful, Nigel, if she really *was* dead, or had fainted?'

185

'Don't be an idiot, Mariella!' said Nigel. 'Of course she's not dead, or anything. You watch – she'll get up and bow ever so gracefully in a minute. They always do!'

'How do you know – you've never seen a ballet. You said so,' I whispered.

'No – but I've seen plays. Chap run through with a sword. Stone dead! Gets up and speaks to the audience straight after. Says how much he's enjoyed playing to such an appreciative audience. Same here!'

'She looks so white,' I said.

'Of course! They've probably dabbed her face with flour on the QT while she's been lying there,' said Nigel.

'Oh, no! They wouldn't do that – not in ballet,' I said, shocked at the very idea. 'And now I come to think about it, someone really *was* stabbed when they were acting in Shakespeare – *Hamlet*, or something. I saw it in the paper!'

'Sh!' Nigel said urgently. People were staring at us indignantly, and Nigel had all the average Englishman's horror of attracting attention to himself. 'I must say that's quite effective!'

'That' was the barrier of climbing roses and flowers that was slowly rising up from the front of the stage, hiding the Sleeping Beauty's palace from our view as the curtain fell.

'Well, I wonder where Jane can have got to?' I said, as the first interval passed and she hadn't yet appeared.

'Oh, I expect she thought it was too far to come all that way round,' said Nigel. 'Fairly big place, this, you know.'

'I expect you're right,' I agreed. 'Or perhaps I mistook what she said, and she'll come in the second interval. By the way, this next act is a Vision of the Princess Aurora. The Lilac Fairy shows the beautiful Princess to the

186

King's son in a vision, and he falls in love with her.'

'Of course!' laughed Nigel. 'They always do – in fairy-tales!'

The curtain rose again, and the beautiful vision scene unfolded before our eyes.

'Isn't she lovely?' I breathed. 'So young and dreamy – quite different from the last scene, which was gay and brilliant. That's as it should be, of course, because this is supposed to be a sort of dream. She *is* lovely – I'd forgotten just how beautiful. She looks awfully young for her age, don't you think?'

'How do I know?' said Nigel. 'How old is the girl, anyway?'

'Oh, Veronica is twenty-three – or is it twenty-four? I forget,' I said, 'but she only looks seventeen on the stage. And now I come to think about it, she's frightfully like Jane. Don't you think so, Uncle Harold?'

Uncle Harold studied the dancer through his glasses.

'Yes, she is,' he agreed. 'But then all dancers look alike to me – especially when they have their hair done in the classical style.'

'Jumping Jehoshaphat!' exclaimed Nigel, taking the glasses in his turn. 'You're right, Mariella! She's the living image of Jane! Gosh – I'll wager a hundred to one she *is* Jane! She's got that look upon her face she always had when she went out riding with me – as if she was somewhere else, if you know what I mean. It used to aggravate me beyond anything. Yes, it's Jane or I'm a Dutchman! Don't you think so, sir?'

He thrust the glasses back into Uncle Harold's hands.

'There certainly *is* an amazing likeness,' Uncle Harold declared. 'But of course it couldn't possibly be Jane. She's watching in the wings – she said so.'

'No, of course it couldn't be Jane.'

But all the same both Nigel and I knew that it *was* Jane, though how it had come about we couldn't possibly imagine. When the second interval came, and still Jane didn't appear, I can't say we were surprised. We knew that somewhere behind the curtain, in the dressing-rooms, Jane was feverishly getting ready for the next act.

The curtain rose, and the Awakening Scene began. When the Prince appeared – it was Josef Linsk, of course – and wakened the sleeping Princess with a kiss, we could hardly conceal our excitement.

'Holy snakes!' exclaimed Nigel, quite forgetting the people round us. 'Look at that! She's wakened up all right! Gosh! I've never seen old Jane look so perky! She must have a crush on the fellow!'

'She's always been keen on Josef Linsk,' I answered. 'Ever since she was a kid of fifteen. It's my opinion she fell in love with him all those years ago at the swimming baths. And now, look at her!'

Entranced, we watched the dazzling creature of dew and fire upon the stage. Now tender, now brilliant, she charmed that vast audience with her every movement.

When, at the end of the performance, Madame, the director of the Covent Garden Company, came on to the stage, holding the Princess Aurora by the hand, and on the other side of the dancer appeared the stage manager, we weren't a bit surprised, because we knew it was Jane. But the rest of the audience was! To its astonishment it learned that its beloved Veronica Weston had collapsed at the end of the first act as the result of influenza. No, no – nothing to worry about! The doctor had already seen her, and all she needed was a complete rest. She was leav-

Entranced, we watched the dazzling creature of dew and fire upon the stage

ing London tomorrow, and next week she was going to be married to Mr Scott who had conducted so brilliantly this evening. There was a burst of clapping at this announcement, though most people knew about Veronica Weston's forthcoming marriage already.

And what about the young, unknown dancer who had stepped from the wings into the principal role at a moment's notice? The audience learned that she was Jane Foster, and that she had been understudying Veronica Weston during the last few weeks. They learned that she was eighteen, and very shy. Not awkward, of course, for no dancer is that, but so shy that she stood there, a little behind Madame, blushing like any schoolgirl.

'But Jane is going to be a very great dancer,' said Madame, drawing her forward a little, and kissing her, whereupon there was another burst of clapping. 'We are going to be very proud of Jane Foster!'

Now this is really the end of my story – the story of Jane's success. As Jane herself said, when we were undressing in her little room at 140a Fortnum Mansions, 'There isn't any more to tell – except that I was so nervous when I first went on tonight that I trembled in every limb! It's a wonder you didn't *see* me trembling, Mariella. I felt as if everyone could see!'

'You looked perfectly all right to me!' I laughed. 'In fact you danced wonderfully. Surely you weren't nervous *all* the time, Jane?'

'Oh, no!' confessed Jane. 'I got that feeling – all stage people know it – that I'd really captured the audience, and after that, strength seemed to pour into my limbs. It was like – well, like a dragonfly coming out of its shroud, and feeling the sun upon its wings. Then I forgot all about those thousands of people, and just danced. You've no idea what a help Josef was. He's wonderful, Mariella, is Josef! He partnered me beautifully.'

I said nothing. Never, never would I really like Josef Linsk – however wonderful he was in Jane's eyes. But, as Daddy said in one of his books, it's a blessing we don't all like the same sort of people! Life would be so dull!

'It's funny,' Jane said with a yawn, 'but I've just remembered something I said years ago, away back in Northumberland, before I came to London. I stood at my window – *your* window now, Mariella – and I looked at the hills and moors, and I turned my back on them, and I can remember saying quite distinctly: "I'm going to be a dancer! I must! I must!" And now look at me! I *am*!'

Lorna Hill
No Castanets at the Wells £2.25

Veronica Western isn't the only one in her family with the dream of being a dancer. Her cousin, Caroline Scott, wins a place at the Sadler's Wells Ballet School, too. But she doesn't have Veronica's natural gift for ballet, and one disappointment just leads to another.

Then Caroline meets a young Spaniard called Angelo Ibanez – and discovers that there's much more to dance than just ballet. Soon her career takes a dramatic turn – leading to fame that she never thought possible!

This and other books are available at your local bookshop or newsagent, or can be ordered direct from the publisher Indicate the number of copies required and fill in the form below

Name_____
(Block letters please)

Address_____

_____

Send to CS Department, Pan Books Ltd.
PO Box 40, Basingstoke, Hants
Please enclose remittance to the value of the cover price plus
60p for the first book plus 30p per copy for each additional book ordered to a
maximum charge of £2.40 to cover postage and packing
Applicable only in the UK

While every effort is made to keep prices low, it is sometimes necessary to
increase prices at short notice. Pan Books reserve the right to show on covers
and charge new retail prices which may differ from those advertised in the text or
elsewhere